F
GIN

8905630

Ginzburg, Natalia
16.45
Voices in the evening

VOICES IN THE EVENING

Also by Natalia Ginzburg

All Our Yesterdays

Family Sayings

The Little Virtues

The City and the House

The Manzoni Family

Valentino and Sagittarius

Family: Family and Borghesia,
Two Novellas

Voices In the Evening

Natalia Ginzburg

Translated from the Italian by D. M. Low

ARCADE PUBLISHING • NEW YORK
Little, Brown and Company

To Gabriele

Originally published in Italian under the title *Le Voci Della Sera*

AUTHOR'S NOTE

The places and characters in this story are imaginary. The first are not found on any map, the others are not alive, nor have ever lived, in any part of the world. I am sorry to say this having loved them as though they were real.

Library of Congress Cataloging-in-Publication Data

Ginzburg, Natalia.
[Voci della sera. English]
Voices in the evening / Natalia Ginzburg; translated from the Italian by D. M. Low.
p. cm.
Translation of: Le voci della sera.
ISBN 1-55970-016-5
I. Title.
PQ4817.I5V613 1963
853'.912 — dc20 89-15081
CIP

Published in the United States by Arcade Publishing, Inc., New York, a Little, Brown company

10 9 8 7 6 5 4 3 2 1

BP

PRINTED IN THE UNITED STATES OF AMERICA

Contents

TRANSLATOR'S NOTE

It is an ancient and wide-spread custom in Italy to give people nicknames by which they are known not only to their intimates, but to the world at large. This is so much so that sometimes few people know a man's real name. Thus in the present work one of the chief characters, De Francisci, is universally known as Balotta, that is Little Ball, and another one as Purillo from the peculiar cap invariably worn by him. This man's surname is only casually revealed towards the end of the book. The real name of a man known as Nebbia, that is Mist, is never mentioned. The meaning of some of these nicknames has been inserted in the translation at their first occurrence.

It is also well known that in Italian, as in several other languages, people on intimate terms address one another in the second person singular. This usage would be out of place in modern English dialogue. Accordingly the plural pronoun and verb have been substituted in this translation without comment. In some places however the use of the second person singular is referred to explicitly in the course of the story. In such places a phrase about 'the familiar form of address' has been inserted in the English text, or one speaker has been made to address another as 'my dear'. The reader will understand that in such places the speaker was using the second person singular.

D.M.L.

VOICES IN THE EVENING

1

Elsa and her Mother and Family

I HAD gone with my mother to the doctor's and we were returning home, by the path which skirts General Sartorio's wood, and the high wall, covered with moss, of the Villa Bottiglia.

It was October, and beginning to be cold: in the village, over our shoulders, the first street lamps had been lit and the blue globe of the Hotel Concordia illuminated the deserted piazza with its glaucous light.

My mother said, 'I feel a kind of lump in my throat. It hurts if I swallow.'

She said, 'Good evening, General.'

General Sartorio had passed us, raising his hat above his silvery waved hair, a monocle in his eye, and his dog on a lead.

My mother said, 'What a fine head of hair he has, at that age!'

She said, 'Did you notice how ugly the dog has become?

'I have a kind of vinegary taste in my mouth now, and that lump hurts me all the time.

'However did he discover that I have high blood pressure? It has always been low with me, always.'

She said, 'Good evening, Gigi.'

General Sartorio's son had passed us with his white montgomery over his shoulders. He was supporting on one arm a salad bowl covered with a napkin. The other arm was in plaster of Paris and in a sling.

'He had a really horrid fall. I wonder if he will ever recover the full use of his arm?' said my mother.

She said, 'I wonder what he had got in that bowl.

'One can see that there is a party somewhere,' she added, 'At the Terenzis' very likely. Everyone who goes has to take something. Nowadays many people do that.'

She said, 'But they don't invite you, do they?

'They don't invite you,' she said, 'because they think that you give yourself airs. You have never been to the tennis club either. If one does not go about and show oneself, people say that such a person is giving himself airs, and they don't seek one out any more. Now, the little Bottiglia girls, on the other hand, everyone invites them. The other evening they danced at the Terenzis' until three in the morning. There were some foreigners there, a Chinese man even.'

The little Bottiglia girls were always so called in our family, although the youngest girl is now twenty-nine.

She said, 'Perhaps I have a little hardening of the arteries, have I, do you think?'

She said, 'Shall we have any faith in the new doctor? The old one was old, of course. He was not interested any more. If one told him of anything wrong, he immediately said he had the same trouble himself. This one writes everything down. Did you notice how he writes everything? Did you see how ugly his wife was?'

She said, 'Couldn't we sometimes have the miracle of a word from you?'

'What wife?' I said.

'The doctor's wife.'

'The one that came to the door,' said I, 'was not his wife. She was the nurse. The tailor at Castello's daughter.'

'The tailor at Castello's daughter! How ugly she is!

'And how was it she had no overall? She will be his servant, not the nurse, you see.'

'She had no overall,' said I, 'because she had taken it off as she was just going. The doctor has neither a maid nor a wife. He is a bachelor and has his meals at the Concordia.'

'A bachelor, is he?'

My mother in her own thoughts immediately married me off with the doctor.

'I wonder if he finds himself better off here than at

Cignano. Better at Cignano, probably. More people, more life. We shall have to ask him to dinner sometime. With Gigi Sartorio.'

'His fiancée,' said I, 'is at Cignano. They are getting married in the spring.'

'Who?'

'The doctor.'

'So young, and already engaged!'

We were walking up our garden path, which was carpeted with leaves. The kitchen window was lit up and our maid Antonia could be seen beating some eggs.

My mother said, 'That lump in my throat is quite dry now; it moves neither up nor down.'

She sat down with a sigh in the hall and was knocking her galoshes together to shake off the mud. My father came to the door of his study with his pipe and the jacket of Pyrenaean wool he wears in the house.

'I have got high blood pressure,' said my mother with a trace of pride.

'High?' said Aunt Ottavia, at the head of the stairs, arranging the two black tresses on her head. They were woolly like a doll's.

'High. Not low. High.'

One of Aunt Ottavia's cheeks was red, the other pale, as always happened when she fell asleep in her armchair by the stove over a book from the 'Selecta' library.

'They sent up from the Villa Bottiglia,' said Antonia from the kitchen doorway, 'for some flour. They had only a little and had to make some *beignets*. I gave them a good bowlful.'

'Again? Why, they are always out of flour. They could do without making *beignets*. They are heavy at night.'

'They are not at all heavy,' said Aunt Ottavia.

'They are heavy.'

My mother took off her hat, her coat and the cat-skin lining which she always wears underneath, then the shawl which she fastens over her breast with a safety pin.

'But perhaps,' she said, 'they have made the *beignets* for the party, which must be at the Terenzis'. We saw Gigi Sartorio, too, with a salad bowl. Who came to ask for the flour? Carola? Didn't she tell you anything about a party?'

'Me, they didn't tell me anything,' said Antonia.

I went up to my room. It is on the top floor, and looks across country. Of an evening one can make out the lights of Castello in the distance, and the scattered ones of Castel Piccolo, high upon the shoulder of the hill, and beyond the hill is the town.

My room has a bed in a recess with muslin curtains, a small low easy chair in mouse-grey velvet, a chest of drawers with a looking glass and a cherry-wood desk.

There is as well a maiolica stove, marron in colour, some logs in a basket, and a revolving bookcase with a plaster wolf on top, made by our man's son who is in an asylum. Hanging on the wall is a reproduction of the *Madonna of the Chair*, a view of St. Mark's, and a sachet for stockings, quite a big one, of point lace with blue love-knots, a present from Signora Bottiglia.

I am twenty-seven.

I have a sister a little older than myself. She is married and lives at Johannesburg, and my mother reads the paper continually to see if they say anything about South Africa. She is always anxious about what is happening down there. In the night she wakes up and says to my father,

'But down there where Teresita is, the Mau Mau will never get there, will they?'

Then I have a brother, rather younger than I am, who works in Venezuela. In the cupboard of the store-room of our house there are still his fencing masks and underwater things and boxing gloves, for as a boy he went in for sport; when the cupboard is flung open the boxing gloves topple down on one's head.

My mother is always lamenting that her children are so far away. She often goes off to have a cry over it with her friend Signora Ninetta Bottiglia.

All the same she gets some satisfaction out of shedding these tears. They feed her self-esteem, since there is mingled with them some pride in having sent her offspring to such remote and perilous places. But my mother's most persistent worry is that I do not get married. This is an annoyance which depresses her, and the only consolation she gets lies in the fact that the little Bottiglia girls at the age of thirty have not got married either.

For a long time my mother cherished the dream that I should marry General Sartorio's son—a dream which vanished when she was told that the General's son was a morphine addict and not interested in women.

Still she takes the idea up again occasionally. She wakes up in the night and says to my father,

'We shall have to invite General Sartorio's son to dinner.'

Then she says, 'But do you believe that he is a pervert, that boy?'

My father says, 'How should I know?'

'They say it of so many and they will be saying it assuredly of our Giampiero.'

'Very likely,' says my father.

'Very likely? How, very likely? Do you actually know that someone has said it?'

'How should I know?'

'Who could have said it, such a thing, of my Giampiero?'

We have lived in the neighbourhood for many years. My father is the accountant of the factory. The lawyer Bottiglia is the manager. The whole neighbourhood lives by the factory.

The factory produces cloth.

It emits a smell which permeates the streets of the town and when the scirocco blows it comes pretty well up to our house, which is, however, in the country. At times the smell is like rotten eggs, at others like curdled milk. There is nothing to be done about it, as it is caused by the chemicals which they use, my father says.

The owners of the factory are the De Francisci.

2

Old Balotta

OLD De Francisci was known as old Balotta or Little Ball. He was short and stout with a big paunch, as round as round, which overflowed above the waist of his trousers, and he had large drooping moustaches discoloured by the cigars which he chewed and sucked. He began with a workshop hardly as big as 'from here to there', my father relates. He went about on his bicycle with an old haversack in which he put his lunch, and he used to eat it leaning against a wall of the yard, covering his jacket with crumbs and draining the wine from the bottle's neck. That wall is still there, and it is known as old Balotta's wall because in the evening after the day's work he used to stand there with his cap on the back of his head smoking a cigar and chatting with his workmen.

My father says, 'When old Balotta was here certain things did not happen.'

Old Balotta was a Socialist. He always remained one, although after the coming of Fascism he dropped his habit of uttering his thoughts aloud. He became in the end melancholy and sullen. When he got up in the morning he would say to his wife Cecilia,

'What a stink, anyway.'

And would add,

'I cannot endure it.'

Signora Cecilia would say,

'You cannot endure the smell from your factory any more?' And he said,

'No, I cannot endure it any more.' And again,

'I cannot go on with this life.'

'It is enough that you are healthy,' said Signora Cecilia.

'You,' said old Balotta to his wife, 'are always saying something fresh and original.'

Later he had trouble with his gall-bladder and said to his wife,

'Now I haven't even got my health, I cannot go on.'

'One goes on until God gives the word,' Signora Cecilia told him.

'Pah! God! We *should* have to bring God into it!'

He still took up his place against the wall in the yard. The wall and that corner of the yard is all that remains of the old workshop. The rest now is a building of reinforced concrete, almost as big as the whole village. But he no longer ate those hunks of bread. The doctor had ordered him a diet of boiled vegetables which he was obliged to eat at home, sitting up to a table; and he had also forbidden him his wine, his cigar and the bicycle. They used to take him to the works in a motor-car.

Old Balotta brought up a boy, a distant relation, who had been left an orphan as a small child, and he had him educated with his own sons. His name is Fausto, but everyone calls him Purillo; because he always wears a beret of the kind called *purillo*, drawn down over his ears. When Fascism came Purillo became a Fascist, and old Balotta said,

'Naturally, because Purillo is like a gold-fly which when it settles settles on dung.'

Old Balotta would be walking up and down the yard of the factory, his hands behind his back, his beret thrust down on the nape of his neck, his greasy worn scarf about his throat, like a piece of rope, and he would stop in front of Purillo, who was now working in the factory and say,

'You, Purillo, are distasteful to me. I cannot bear you.'

Purillo would grin, curling his small mouth and showing his fine white teeth; he would spread out his arms and say,

'I cannot possibly be to everyone's taste.'

'True,' said old Balotta, and he would walk away with his hands behind his back, with his shambling gait, shuffling his shoes as though they were slippers.

However, when he began to be ill, he named Purillo as manager of the factory.

Signora Cecilia gave herself no peace over this affront to her sons.

'Why Purillo?' she asked. 'Why not Mario? Why not Vincenzo?'

But old Balotta said,

'Don't you push yourself in here. Push yourself into your sauces. Purillo has a good brain. Your sons are not worth a fig. Purillo has a fine brain even if I cannot bear him.' And he added,

'Only, everything will go to the dogs with this war.'

Purillo had always lived with them at La Casetta, as old Balotta's villa was called. He had bought it for a small sum, at the time of the first war. When he bought it, it had been a peasant's house with a kitchen garden, orchard and vineyard. Later he enlarged and embellished it with a veranda and balconies, preserving at the same time something of its rustic appearance. So Purillo had always lived with them, until one fine day old Balotta turned him out. Purillo went to live at Le Pietre on the other side of the hill, which old Balotta had bought for his brother and sister, Barba Tommaso and Magna Maria, a house which old Balotta regarded in a way as a place of exile to which he banished his sons at various times when there was too much quarrelling. But when he sent Purillo there it was clear that it was final. The evening that he had gone away Signora Cecilia burst into tears at table, not that she had any special affection for Purillo, but she felt not having him any more in the house where she had always had him from a baby. Old Balotta said,

'You won't waste your tears over Purillo, will you? I am eating my supper better without that ugly snout.'

Neither Barba Tommaso nor Magna Maria was asked if they were ready to have Purillo with them. But in any case old Balotta never asked either of them for their consent or opinion on any matter.

He used to say,

'My brother Barba Tommaso, speaking with all respect, is a ninny.

'My sister Magna Maria, speaking with all respect, is a half wit.'

Nor, of course, was Purillo asked either if he liked being with Barba Tommaso and Magna Maria.

However, Purillo spent very little time with these two old people. He took his meals with them and after dinner brought out a snakeskin case with his initials in gold on it.

'Cigarette, Barba Tommaso?'

'Cigarette, Magna Maria?'

He never troubled himself to say anything else.

He pulled his beret over his head and went off to the works.

Barba Tommaso and Magna Maria feared and respected him. They did not dare say a word when he hung up a large photograph of himself in the dining-room wearing a black shirt and raising his arm to the salute among some Party officers who had come to visit the works.

Barba Tommaso and Magna Maria had never had any definite political opinions. Still they would whisper to one another,

'If Balotta comes here one day, what will happen then?'

That was in any case an improbable eventuality. Old Balotta never came to Le Pietre.

Then the war came. Balotta's sons went on service, but Purillo was not called up because he had some constriction of the throat or chest—and he had had pleurisy as a child and a murmur could still be heard on one side.

After the Eighth of September Purillo came one night to wake up Balotta and Signora Cecilia. He told them to dress at once and come away, because the Fascists were intending to come and get them. Balotta protested and said he would not move. He said that everyone in the neighbourhood liked him and no one would venture to do anything to him. But Purillo with a face like marble had seized a suitcase and stood there with his hands on his belt saying,

'We mustn't lose time. Put some things in this and let us go.'

Thereupon old Balotta got up and began to dress. He fumbled over his braces and buttons with his freckled hands that were covered with white wrinkled skin.

'Where are we going?' he said.

'To Cignano.'

'To Cignano, to Cignano! And to whose house?'

'I am thinking.'

Signora Cecilia, in her alarm, wandered round the rooms picking up at random what she found there, some flower vases which she put in a bag, silver spoons and old camisoles.

Purillo got them into a motor-car. He drove without saying a word, with his long beaky nose curving over his black bristling moustache, his little mouth tight shut, his cap drawn over his ears.

'You, Purillo,' said old Balotta, 'are probably saving my life. All the same, you are distasteful to me, and I cannot bear you.'

And Purillo this time said,

'I am not bound to be to your taste.'

'That is true,' said old Balotta.

Purillo always spoke formally to old Balotta, because Balotta had never told him to say *thou*.

At Cignano, Purillo had rented a small apartment for them. They passed the days in the kitchen, where the stove was. Purillo came to see them almost every evening.

The Fascists did actually come to La Casetta and they broke the windows and ripped up the chairs with bayonets.

Signora Cecilia died at Cignano. She had struck up a friendship with the landlady, and passed away holding her hand. Old Balotta had gone to find a doctor. When he returned with one his wife was dead.

He just could not believe it, and went on speaking to her and shaking her. He thought she had merely fainted.

Only he and Purillo were at the funeral, and the lady who owned the house. Barba Tommaso and Magna Maria were ill, with fever.

'Funk fever,' said old Balotta.

Purillo did not appear there any more. So Balotta was alone, though he seemed to want Purillo. Every minute he was asking the landlady,

'But where has Purillo run off to?'

It became known that Purillo had escaped to Switzerland, having been threatened with death either by the Fascists or by the Partisans. The factory remained entirely on the shoulders of an old surveyor, one Borzaghi. But the factory meant nothing any more to old Balotta.

His memory began to fail somewhat. He often fell asleep on a chair in the kitchen with his head bowed. He would wake up with a start and ask the landlady,

'Where are my children?'

He asked her this with a threatening air as though she had got them hidden from him in the store-room cupboard.

'The boys, the grown-up ones, are at the war,' said the landlady. 'Don't you remember that they are at the war? Little Tommasino is at school; and the girls, Gemmina is in Switzerland and Raffaella is in the mountains with the Partisans.'

'What a life!' said old Balotta.

And then he went to sleep again, bending forward, and starting up from time to time and looking round with his lack-lustre eyes like one who did not know where he was.

After the Liberation, Magna Maria came to take him away in a car, with the chauffeur. He recognized him, as he was the son of one of his workmen, and embraced him. He held out two flabby fingers to Magna Maria, looking askance at her.

He said,

'You didn't come to Cecilia's funeral.'

'I was in quarantine,' said Magna Maria.

They took him to La Casetta. Magna Maria had cleared away the broken glass and tidied up the rooms a little with the peasant woman's help. But there were no mattresses or sheets, no plate or china. Complete devastation existed in the garden, just where once upon a time one saw Signora Cecilia moving about in the midst of her roses, with her blue apron, her scissors attached to her belt, and her watering pot in her hand.

Old Balotta went away with Magna Maria to Le Pietre. Barba Tommaso was there just the same as ever, rosy faced in his clean shirt and white flannel trousers.

Old Balotta came and sat down and suddenly began sobbing into his handkerchief, like a little child.

Magna Maria stroked his head and kept on repeating, 'Splendid, splendid. You are splendid. How splendid you are!'

Barba Tommaso said,

'I was the first to see the Partisans come. I was at the window with my telescope; General Sartorio was there, too. I saw them approaching up the road. I went to meet them with two bottles of wine, because I guessed they were thirsty.'

And he said,

'At the factory, the Germans have carried off all the machinery. But it does not matter, because now the Americans will give us new machinery.'

Old Balotta said,

'You just keep quiet. What a ninny you always are!'

'Borghazi was very brave,' said Magna Maria. 'The Germans arrested him, but he threw himself out of the train as it was going, and fractured his shoulder.'

And she said,

'You know that they killed Nebbia?'

'Nebbia?'

'Why yes. The Fascists took him and killed him, just there at the back, on those rocks there. It was at night and we heard him cry out. And in the morning our woman found his scarf, and his spectacles all broken, and his cap, that fur one which he always wore.'

Old Balotta was looking at the setting sun above the sloping rocks behind the house which is for that reason called Le Pietre, and at the clumps of pine trees which cover that side of the hill, and beyond the hills at the mountains with their sharp snowy peaks, and the long blue shadows of the glaciers and a white sugar-loaf summit, known as Lo Scivolo, 'the Slide', where his children used to go on Sundays with their friends.

The following day the mayor came to invite him to make a speech in honour of the Liberation. They brought him out on the balcony of the town hall and below was a large crowd, the whole piazza was full. There were people also right down the street, they had climbed up the trees and telegraph poles. He recognized faces, some of his workmen, but he felt shy about speaking. He leaned with his hands on the balustrade and said,

'Viva il Socialismo!'

Then he remembered Nebbia. He took off his beret and said,

'Viva il Nebbia!'

Loud applause broke out like the roll of thunder; and he was rather frightened and then suddenly felt very happy.

Then he wanted to speak again, but he did not know what else to say. He gasped and fumbled with his coat collar. They led him from the balcony, because now the mayor was to speak.

While they were on their way home Barba Tommaso said to him,

'Nebbia was never a Socialist, he was a Communist.'

'No matter,' said old Balotta, 'and you shut up, what a ninny you always are!'

At home again, Magna Maria put him to bed. He

was flushed and fevered and had difficulty with his breathing.

He died in the night.

In the neighbourhood they said what a tragedy—that old Balotta is dead. Who knows what has become of his children, and the factory is left in Purillo's hands.

They said,

'All those children and not one of them here at the moment of his death.'

The day after he died his younger daughter Raffaella appeared, the one who had been in the mountains with the Partisans. She was wearing trousers, a red handkerchief round her neck, and a pistol in a holster.

She was eager for her father to see her with that pistol. She came to Le Pietre and found Magna Maria at the garden gate with black crepe on her head. Maria began to cry and said,

'What a tragedy—what a tragedy!'

Then she embraced Raffaella and said

'How splendid you are! Yes, splendid, splendid!' and added,

'But don't you ever fire that pistol here.'

3

Elsa and her Family

DURING the war we went away first to Castello and then to Castel Piccolo for fear that the village would be bombed because of the factory.

My mother kept chickens at Castello and turkeys and rabbits, and had also started a colony of bees. But there must have been something wrong with the hives, because the bees died, the whole lot of them, when the snow came.

At Castel Piccolo she would not have any more animals. She said that when she had to look after animals she became fond of them and she could not bear cooking them any more.

Now we have various animals at our dairy farm. This is called La Vigna and lies in the direction of the woods of Castello about a kilometre from us. My mother goes to La Vigna two or three times every week. But she does not make friends with the animals. The woman on the farm looks after them and Antonia kills, plucks or skins them, and my mother puts them all in the pot without troubling herself, because she does not stop to think that they once had feathers or skins.

After the Liberation my sister was called on to be an interpreter, because she had a good knowledge of English. An American colonel fell in love with her and they got married and went off to Johannesburg. In civil life he had a business down there.

I went to the university in the town. I lived together with the younger of the little Bottiglia girls at the Protestant Centre. Giuliana Bottiglia completed her teachers' training and I took a degree in literature and then we both returned home.

About twice every week I go to town on one pretext or another—to change the books at the 'Selecta' library for Aunt Ottavia, to buy threads for my mother's embroidery or a special brand of English tobacco for my father.

I usually go on the motor-bus which leaves at midday from the piazza and get off in the Corso Piacenza in the town two steps away from the Via dello Statuto, where the 'Selecta' library is.

The last bus is at ten o'clock in the evening.

I was in the little arm-chair. I pressed my hands against the sides of the stove and took them away when I felt them burning and put them to my face, and then put them on the stove again. And so I whiled away half an hour.

Giuliana Bottiglia appeared.

She was wearing black stockings, as was the fashion at that time, and black leather gloves, a very short white raincoat and a black silk scarf on her head.

'Am I disturbing you?' she said.

She sat down and took off her gloves and scarf and began to comb her wavy hair. Then she shook it out; it is black and fluffed out, with little curls, like commas, on the temples.

'I went to the cinema today,' she said, 'at Cignano.'

'What were they doing?'

'*Fiery Darkness*.'

'But why was the darkness fiery?'

'Because He was an engineer—gone blind,' she said, 'and She was a woman off the streets, but He did not know that and believed She was pure and they get married. They take a very fine apartment. But He begins to have his suspicions.'

'Why suspicions?'

'Because She had told him that previously She had been poor, and instead He discovers that She was by no means so poor, since She has a good deal of jewellery. He discovers that because the maid tells him she had seen her with the jewellery.'

'Previously?'

'Yes, previously. And one evening He hears her talking to someone on the terrace. This is a banker very much enamoured of her who knows about her past, and is blackmailing her. He tells her that either She makes love with him or if not he goes to the blind man and tells him everything. The banker is Yul Brynner.'

'The one with the shaven head?'

'Yes. Then the engineer decides to have an operation which either kills him or restores his sight. Well, they do it and He gets his sight; at first all is confused, and then clear, and She is there looking lovely with an ermine cape. And He takes the cape in his arms and cries.'

'Cries?'

'Yes. Then they go to a villa for a holiday, but Yul Brynner comes, too. And in the night Brynner looks for her and at last finds her in a little room, with some books, a sort of library. And he wants to kill her, and the engineer comes in and finds them together.'

'And then?'

'Then the end is that Yul Brynner runs away with the engineer after him and they are on a window ledge. She, too, has got on to the ledge to save the engineer and then She falls off it.'

'Killed?'

'Yes.'

'And the engineer?'

'The engineer fires at the banker and he dies. But before he dies in the hospital he tells the engineer that She was as innocent as a saint. And the engineer goes blind again.'

'Goes blind again?'

'Yes.'

'Why does he go blind again?'

'Because his eyes were still weak, and, you see, the retina becomes detached through shock.'

'It was an idiotic film.'

'Not at all. They did it well.'

'And you went to Cignano to see it?'

'To Cignano, yes.'

'By bus?'

'No, on my bicycle with my sister Maria and Maria Mosso.'

'Was the Chinese man nice?'

'What Chinese man?'

'The one at the dance at the Terenzis'.'

'He wasn't Chinese, he was an Indian, and he was at least seventy. Gigi Sartorio brought him.'

She was smoothing her gloves on her lap, gently, gently, with her eyes lowered and her head a bit on one side, and she said,

'Tommasino was there.'

'Where?'

'At the Terenzis' dance.'

'He was?'

'Yes, he was.'

'And—well?'

'Nothing. He was there, that's all.'

She continued to smooth her gloves without looking at me, and said,

'You do not tell me anything any more. I used to be your friend.'

I stirred the ash in the stove and said,

'I don't tell you anything, about what?'

'I come here, we talk about silly little things. I bore you, I know it.'

'You don't bore me at all. I was amused by the story of the engineer.'

'I bore you, I know it.'

She pulled on her gloves, and fastened the belt of her raincoat.

'I must be going now.'

At the door, without turning round, she said,

'They saw you!'

'What?'

'They saw you, with Tommasino.'

'Who did?'

'My sister Maria and Maria Mosso. They saw you both in a bar.'

'And then?'

'Oh, nothing.'

'Giuliana! What is the party at the Terenzis'?' cried my mother at the foot of the stairs.

'I don't know.'

'Because we met Gigi Sartorio with a salad bowl.'

'But he was not going to the Terenzis', he was going to the Mossos' to take them some *zabaione* because they had made so much—what was left over. They gave us some as well.'

'But how much had they made? A barrel?' said my mother.

She said, 'What an idea to put the *zabaione* in a salad bowl.'

'And where should they put it?' said Aunt Ottavia.

'In a glass dish, good gracious!'

'We made some *beignets*,' said Giuliana, 'as we do not care for *zabaione* by itself.'

'We, on the contrary,' said my mother, 'like eating very lightly in the evening.'

One could read in her expression her annoyance because we had been excluded from the little *zabaione* party.

4

Balotta's Children

BALOTTA had five children.

The eldest is Gemmina. She is now over forty; she has not married and lives at La Casetta. When she came back from Switzerland she said,

'No one is going to take La Casetta away from me.'

Her brothers and sister wanted to come and live there after they had all returned to the district; but she repeatedly said,

'La Casetta was Mama's and Papa's and no one is going to take it from me.'

It was useless to point out to her that Mama and Papa were Mama and Papa to the others, and not merely to her.

Gemmina remained at La Casetta, on her own, with one servant, an old nurse who had brought up all the brothers and sisters one after the other.

Vincenzo and Mario wanted to have her, too, as nurse when they had children.

But Gemmina said,

'No one takes nurse away from me. Nurse stays

with me and anyone who interferes with her can look out for himself.'

Gemmina is tall and thin. Her peroxide hair is cut short. Her face is long and narrow, all chin. Her complexion is mottled. An old rash she had once has left livid marks.

In the winter she wears a Casentino overcoat, a beret of shaggy fur, and ski-ing trousers. She is always busy and runs backwards and forwards on her motor-scooter from Castello to Cignano, and from Cignano to Castello. She has started a hospital at Castello and an arts and crafts shop at Cignano. In the window are displayed knitted slippers, boxes of inlaid wood and pictures of Alpine subjects.

She buys apples for the hospital on her way through Soprano, where they are cheap.

Her greatest delight is in organizing charity teas. She gets eight or ten girls going and sends one to Magna Maria to make her give some nuts of which they have plenty at Le Pietre. These are to stick in the cheese rolls. Another girl is sent to the baker at Cignano to beg for broken biscuits which can be ground in a coffee mill and made into a paste with some cocoa. The result is some little cakes, not at all nice, but eatable all the same.

She is mean and does not contribute anything of her own, either money or anything else. She manages to make everyone give her money and things for her hospital and her other enterprises.

All the same, she does go and fish out various little things at home, which she does not know what to do with, for raffles and cotillons—cardboard Easter eggs, silk linings, heart-shaped corkscrews, and pincushions.

When she started the hospital she used to be there of a morning to supervise the work, in her Casentino overcoat, with her nose inflamed by the cold, which also made the marks on her face still more livid, her mountaineering boots, and a cigarette in an onyx holder.

She is fond of receptions and parties. On such occasions she turns out very smartly, with her beaver cape, jewellery and one of the various evening dresses which she has made in the town by a good dressmaker.

She likes meeting contessas at these parties, because she is, in fact, a snob.

She is always running to and fro from morning till evening. She stops for a chat with everybody, because she knows everybody in the district, and to everyone she says closing her eyes and snorting,

'I am worn out.'

She gets home late, and throws herself on the sofa with a pillow under her legs to help her circulation.

She says, 'I am worn out.'

She stays there with her eyes closed, trying to relax, and not to think of anything; for she has read in a magazine that relaxing gives the skin a rest.

'Nurse, the hot-water bottle, and my account-book.'

In comes the nurse with soft steps; she is stout and bent and wears a starched white apron. Her unvaryingly dour countenance is brown and wrinkled like leather.

Gemmina begins turning the leaves of the account-book. Here are the records of her transactions, complicated operations of spending and receiving.

Old Balotta considered her by no means stupid, and used to say she was cut out for business. Only he added,

'Pity she has no sex appeal. And then she has a very bad complexion. Pity she did not take after her mother, who was as fresh as a rose when she was young.'

Gemmina fell in love with Nebbia.

This caused her distress, because love made her still thinner and plainer. In order to be pleasing to him she tinted her cheeks and lips scarlet. She did it badly, without skill, because she only learnt to make up much later in Switzerland, where she had a friend who worked in a beauty parlour. She used too dark a powder, almost marron, to hide the marks on her skin.

She used to wait for him every evening at the gates of the factory, and everyone knew that she was waiting for Nebbia. Nebbia alone had not understood this, because he was simple-minded and stupid about love and his thoughts were elsewhere.

Nebbia would come out with his fanlike ears, his tortoise-shell spectacles, and his big serious mouth.

'What are you doing here?' he would say. 'Your father left some time ago.'

She would say,

'Are you going to give me a lift?'

He put her on the bracket of his bicycle and took her home. He would leave her at some distance from La Casetta at the foot of the path, and remount his machine.

She would say,

'Are we going to the mountains on Sunday?'

'Of course.'

They used to go alone sometimes and sometimes with her brothers and sister or with Purillo or other employees at the works. She had taken lessons in rock-climbing one summer in the Dolomites. She was proud of being courageous, of never having known fear, of never being left behind or of suffering from mountain sickness.

'You have got the wind of a horse,' Nebbia told her.

So they used to go sometimes by themselves, and on one occasion they were caught by a storm and had to take shelter behind a rock and spend the night there.

They put on all the woollies they had. He had a waterproof rug in a bag and they wrapped it round their legs. They drank a little brandy and Nebbia went off in a deep sleep.

She, on the other hand, could not close an eye. She could hear the peals of thunder and the wind whistling across the glacier, and every now and then a fall of stones. She gazed at Nebbia, fast asleep, with his long face, and his big mouth shut, looking so serious. His lips were cracked with the cold and greasy with vaseline.

In the morning the sun came out and Nebbia began to collect the remains of their provisions, the cups and things and the iron crampons.

'Down at the double,' he said. 'Your people will be wondering.'

She felt quite done, frozen, and longed to cry. But she said nothing and pulled on her woollen gauntlets, blowing into them to warm them.

He made fast the rope to her waist, and then to himself, took up his rucksack and they began the descent.

Once below the rocks they plunged down over the pastures at the double. Their packs danced on their shoulders.

They met the rescue party sent out for them by Balotta. It included Vincenzino, Mario and Purillo. At La Casetta, Signora Cecilia was in tears, convinced that they were dead.

Gemmina plunged into a hot bath. She heard her mother in the next room saying,

'I don't let Gemmina go again, not alone with Nebbia. He runs her into too much danger, and then they talk in the village—always on expeditions alone, she and Nebbia.'

Old Balotta said,

'That's the way nowadays, and there is nothing odd about it. Nowadays people go off alone on trips, or climbing, everywhere, a girl and a man. It is the fashion of the times. You can never go against the times.'

He added,

'Both of them have a passion for mountains. I expect he is going to marry her. If he does, I shall be very glad of it.'

But Gemmina in her bathwrap on a stool in the bathroom was in tears. For they had spent the night side by side, she and Nebbia, on a hand's breadth of rock, and he had not even given her a kiss.

Her people saw her come to the table, her eyes all swollen with weeping, and believed that she was suffering from shock through fright and weariness.

Nebbia sometimes came to supper with them. He would discuss affairs at the works with Old Balotta and was always contradicting him; for Nebbia never took advice from anyone in the world. Soon after, Balotta would go to bed, being accustomed to turning in early; and Nebbia remained with Gemmina and Signora Cecilia while they worked at their knitting. But he too, little by little, fell asleep with his long red face on the back of the arm-chair and his big mouth occasionally smiling in his slumbers.

He was famous, Nebbia was, for falling asleep after supper.

'Forgive me if I have been asleep,' he would say, smoothing his curly hair, and picking up his hat and raincoat.

Gemmina would go with him to the garden gate, and he jumped on his bicycle and went off in the direction of the Hotel Concordia, where he lodged.

One evening they were left by themselves, Gemmina and Nebbia, because Balotta had gone to bed and Signora Cecilia and Rafaella were spending the night in the town. Gemmina laid aside her knitting, pushed her hair off her forehead and said,

'I believe, Nebbia, I am in love with you.'

Then she hid her face in her hands and began to cry.

Nebbia was bewildered. His ears were burning, and

he swallowed. His big curved mouth was still a bit cracked with the cold.

'I am sorry,' he said.

Then there was a long silence, and Gemmina cried all the time. He got out his handkerchief, a big crumpled thing, rather dirty, and dried her tears.

He said in a very low voice, hoarsely,

'I have a great affection for you. But I don't feel that I love you.'

They remained sitting there for a while longer without saying anything further. Gemmina was biting her thumbnail, and every now and again sobbed. Then suddenly Balotta appeared, in his pyjamas, to look for his newspaper, and Nebbia quickly thrust his handkerchief back in his pocket and Gemmina took up her knitting needles.

After that Nebbia put his raincoat on, pulled his worn fur cap over his head and went away.

He became engaged a little while after that to the chemist's daughter at Castello. A girl they nicknamed Pupazzina, Little Dolly. She was only nineteen, and was a little plump thing with a headful of curls. She always wore rather full dainty blouses with her waist gripped in a broad belt of black patent leather, and tottered about on very high heels. She wanted a motor-car at once, being anxious to play the lady, and a home with ultra-modern furniture and large plants on the window sills. She could not bear the mountains, either in winter or summer, and felt the cold badly. She was no good on a bicycle. What she liked was dancing, and she married Nebbia who could not dance.

Old Balotta always had a grudge against Nebbia because he had married that goose, and would not have either of his daughters, neither Gemmina nor Raffaella.

Gemmina decided to go away to Switzerland. She had a woman friend there, and obtained work in a travel agency.

She only returned after the war. Pupazzina and the two children she had had by Nebbia had gone away to live at Saluzzo.

Gemmina would never go and see the spot where they had murdered Nebbia on the rocky slope behind Le Pietre.

Sometimes while she was going alone on her motor-scooter she would sing a song which went like this:

Linda, Linda, my only true love,
You're cosy indoors, I've the heavens above!
You're cosy indoors with a beefsteak before you,
I'm stamping outside in the frost! I adore you,
Linda, Linda, my only true love,
You're cosy indoors, I've the heavens above!

This was one they used to sing in chorus, she and Nebbia and Vincenzino and Purillo in the motor-bus on their return from the mountains.

Nebbia used to sing out of tune. She seemed to hear him still. When she sang this song she recalled all her youth, the cheerful evenings when they were coming back from the mountains, their fatigue, the smell of wool and leather, the melted snow under their boots, her shoulders chafed by the straps of the rucksack, the chocolate half finished in the metal container, the oranges, and the wine.

She has never gone back to the mountains. She still keeps in a box a battered tin cup. It is the one out of which they had both drunk, she and Nebbia, the night of the storm.

After Gemmina came Vincenzino. Then Mario, Raffaella, and last Tommasino. Such, you see, were Balotta's children.

Vincenzino was a plump little fair boy, curly as a lamb. He was always dirty and untidy, always had long ringlets over his neck, the pockets of his raincoat were full of small books and newspapers, his shoes undone, because he was no good at tying knots, and the bottoms of his trousers were caked with mud as the result of his rambles in the country.

Old Balotta used to say,

'He looks to me like a little rabbi.'

He would roam the country on his own. At times he would come to a standstill in front of a wall or a gate where one could only see clumps of nettles or tufts of maidenhair; he would stare and stare, and one could not understand what he was staring at.

He used to walk slowly, occasionally pulling a book or a paper out of his pocket which he set about reading as he walked, rather bent, and frowning. Whenever he opened a book it seemed as if he plunged into it nose first.

He was fond of music and had countless wind instruments in his room. At nightfall he would begin to play an oboe, clarinet or flute.

There issued from this a most lamentable wailing, weak and plaintive, like the bleating of sheep. Old Balotta would say,

'Have I always got to hear him bleating like this?'

Vincenzino did not get on very well at school. He had extra coaching all the year round, yet they always ploughed him. Purillo and Mario, younger than he, went ahead, and he was always left behind.

One could never really understand how that could be, seeing that he read so many books, and knew a world of things.

He always spoke in a low voice, with an indistinct burr. He would answer the simplest questions with confused and rambling explanations which faded away slowly on the sad wave of that burr.

His father would say,

'I cannot put up with him.'

And when he listened at dusk to the wailing of the flute he would add,

'If he goes on bleating like that, I send him to Le Pietre.'

And he did send him to Le Pietre for a while. Later he had him back again because he wanted to see for himself what he was made of.

'He can't be absolutely stupid,' he said to his wife.

He took him to the factory and confronted him with the machinery. Vincenzino stared gloomily, his eyes starting out of his head, bending a little and knitting his brows.

He stared hard and his nostrils curled, exactly as sometimes when out of doors he stared at a wall, a tree or a clump of nettles.

He went to school at Salice, to the college. When he had finally obtained his leaving-certificate he went to the university in the town.

His father wanted him to enrol in the Faculty of Economics as Mario had done, who was already in his second year. Instead he enrolled himself like Purillo in Engineering.

He had been determined on this point. Balotta shrugged his shoulders and said to his wife,

'He will never manage to finish the Polytechnic course. Too difficult. But it is his look-out. I really cannot argue with him. He is mad, and you cannot argue with madmen.'

He, Purillo and Mario lived in furnished rooms with a woman to look after them.

Purillo slept with this woman.

She was a fat heavy creature, no longer young. Shut up in his own room, Vincenzino could hear through the wall Purillo's clear laughter and the woman scolding him in a lazy motherly manner.

Vincenzino hated Purillo.

He came to know Nebbia at the Polytechnic. They always saw each other at lectures. They got talking one evening on the train which was taking them home for the week-end. Nebbia's family also lived outside the town.

Vincenzino spoke first, in his low voice. He mentioned that he had a cousin Purillo with whom he lived and whom he hated. He related what Purillo was like, how he washed and ate and made love with the servant, and how he did his exercises in the morning in shorts of black webbing.

Nebbia strained his ear to listen to that long melancholy murmur. He laughed, really because he was amused by such hatred which had no real motive, but ostensibly at Purillo's way of eating and of scratching his armpits, and the physical jerks up and down in a rowing vest and shorts.

He knew Purillo by sight. When he came to know him personally he thought him quite harmless. Nebbia was in any case sociable and simple-minded. He was quiet and reserved and got on well with everybody.

Vincenzino struck up a friendship with Nebbia; he was his first and last and only friend.

Nebbia took him to his home, in Borgo Martino, and introduced him to his parents, his father a panel doctor, his mother a schoolmistress, and to his brothers and sisters.

Vincenzino in turn brought him to La Casetta.

Nebbia appealed to old Balotta—who even promised him a place in the factory when he should have finished at the Polytechnic.

They went climbing on Sundays all together: Nebbia, Vincenzino, Nebbia's sisters, Gemmina and Purillo. Vincenzino walked slowly and lagged behind; the others got impatient through having to wait for him. So he usually stopped at a rest hut by the fire, to bleat on his flute and stare at the flames.

One summer at San Remo he got to know a girl from Brazil who was studying music. He was at the seaside there on his doctor's advice after tonsilitis; but he did not swim, or sunbathe on the beach, because his skin was so white and delicate that the sun gave him a temperature, and in any case he hated the sun and the sand and the beach umbrellas and the crowd. Consequently he stayed reading under the trees in the hotel garden, and so got into conversation with the girl from Brazil, who did not bathe either and wore dark glasses and a big sun hat. She had her mother with her, *La Mamita*, a little old lady rather like a monkey, with red-dyed hair.

Vincenzino returned to La Casetta from the sea quite restored to health. He placed a portrait on the table in his room. It showed a girl standing up, in profile, wearing evening dress with a rope of pearls. She had a long neck, a huge black chignon and a feather boa.

'My fiancée,' he said.

Balotta said to his wife, 'Is he engaged, that clown there?'

He went to look at the portrait when Vincenzino was out.

'What a long neck,' he said.

And in the morning when he was hardly awake he said to his wife,

'That young woman will cover him with horns from his head to his feet and from his feet to his head.'

Vincenzino wrote long letters to Sao Paolo in Brazil, and received correspondingly long ones, closely written in a big pointed hand. They were difficult to read, being written on the back of the sheet as well.

Towards Christmas the girl arrived in the town with *Mamita, Papito* and *Fifito*, her twelve-year-old brother. They meant to be taken up to La Casetta and to get to know Vincenzino's family.

They stayed at the hotel and Vincenzino took them round to see the town.

One evening on coming home Purillo found Vincenzino on his bed, white as a sheet, and being sick into a basin. He was quivering all over and had had a nervous shock.

He had realized that he was sick to death of *Mamita, Papito, Fifito* and the girl, and could not see how to disentangle himself from them.

Purillo went to get a doctor and Nebbia. They stayed there all night, he and Nebbia, to look after Vincenzino; made him drink some strong coffee and mopped his brow for him.

Next morning they went to see *Papito* and *Mamita* and told them that Vincenzino was ill, very ill, and for the time being could not think of getting married.

Mamita began to cry. Then they asked for money.

They had had travelling expenses and had bought a costly trousseau for their daughter.

They got all they wanted and left again for Brazil.

'Purillo,' so Vincenzino told Nebbia, 'behaved very well.'

But Vincenzino felt no gratitude towards Purillo. On the contrary, because he had been seen by him in such a plight, he disliked him more than ever.

Purillo appeared very kind and sad about it when he reported the affair to old Balotta. But there was a trace of irrepressible delight in his voice. He, Purillo, used to run after the girls all right, and went to bed with prostitutes and servants. But he had never got into any trouble; it had never fallen to old Balotta to pay up for any of his adventures in love.

Vincenzino was sent to the sea once more, because he was ill again. But this time Gemmina went with him to see that he did not commit any fresh follies.

He left the Polytechnic, being too far behind with his examinations, and enrolled himself for Economics and Commerce.

Meanwhile Nebbia had taken his degree some time ago and was working at the factory. Purillo and Mario had also graduated and were working there.

Then Vincenzino's turn came to do his military service. They sent him to Pesaro. He was always being confined to barracks, as he was totally incapable of punctuality and smartness. He had let his beard grow, and his cheeks were covered with a curly rosy sort of hair like some wild plant which grows on a deserted river bank.

Finally, when his time was up, he obtained his degree.

'The last to get there was Gambastorta,' said old Balotta calling him 'Crookshank'. He was pleased, however, and sent him to America for a year, to see the world and learn English.

When Vincenzino returned from America he was greatly changed. To begin with, he no longer had a beard. He had learned to wash himself, and to stand more upright and to speak more loudly.

If one introduced someone new to him, he braced his shoulders and fixed him with a sharp penetrating gaze, brilliant as a flash of cold light.

Sometimes he emitted a quick, sly, secretive laugh which displayed his little white teeth, and died away unexpectedly.

In America he had visited some factories and got new ideas. He wanted to knock their old factory down and rebuild it entirely with large windows, and to add living quarters for the operatives.

He had read books on psychoanalysis, and had discovered that he had a father-complex, and also had experienced a trauma in his infancy on seeing Purillo stone a dog.

He came back to La Casetta and began to work at the factory. He worked late into the night, drawing plans.

His father would say,

'Formerly he took no interest at all in the factory. Now he wants to involve himself in it too much. The sole gain is that he has not got his flute and does not bleat any more.'

However, Vincenzino still went off by himself for walks in the country. And he still stopped to stare motionless at a wall or a tree, frowning and turning up his nose.

He married a girl from Borgo Martino. She was a friend of Nebbia's sisters and he had known her for years. He married her after a complicated and confused declaration of love, and he married her in haste for fear of changing his mind.

One could not see the most distant resemblance between Mario and Vincenzo.

Mario was a cheerful boy, animated and worldly, and everything came to him easily.

Tall, self-possessed, well turned out, he divided his days well enough between work and amusement. After hours he came back to La Casetta to change, and went off to the Sartorios' to play tennis in flannel trousers and a blue jacket with gilt buttons.

'Just like Barba Tommaso. Let us hope that he is not a ninny,' old Balotta would say.

Mario spent his evenings playing poker at the Sartorios', the Peregos' and the Bottiglias'.

He was very good at telling amusing stories, ever so seriously without batting an eyelid. He knew a great many of these, culling them from Italian or foreign magazines to which he subscribed, and he was a great success.

Only at times when he was tired he was subject to nervous bouts of rapid babbling loquaciousness. It was unrestrainable and one could not make him keep quiet. He would tell his stories and make plans for the factory. His face became grey and hollow like a bundle of muscles on the stretch, and he had a little twitching just under his left eye above the cheekbone. At such times he was unable to sleep and passed the nights smoking in his room, or went for a walk in the neighbourhood, and would go as far as Le Pietre to wake up Barba Tommaso and Purillo with his babbling.

They sent him for a while to the sea or to the mountains for a rest, and when he came back he was quite calm again and his insomnia and talkativeness had disappeared.

It looked at one moment as if he was going to get engaged to the elder of the little Bottiglia girls, because he was always going about with her. Instead he went to Munich for some months on business and there he married.

Old Balotta was furious when he knew that he was getting married. The girl was a painter and sculptor, a Russian, her family having escaped from Moscow during the revolution. She was an orphan and lived at Munich with an uncle and aunt. Old Balotta thought that she must be an adventuress or a spy.

He sent Purillo to Munich to see. Purillo gave him to understand that there was nothing to be done; Mario was in love, was getting married and would not listen to reason.

Purillo had picked up some information. The uncle and aunt owned a small shop for records. One understood it was nothing very great.

Mario came to La Casetta with his wife. She was small, thin and harassed-looking. Her face was so powdered that she looked dusty. She wore a black felt hat and black gloves.

When she took her gloves off there appeared two thin, slender hands covered with scars. Mario explained that she had burnt herself with acids while she was preparing her colours, because she always prepared them on her own.

She did not speak a word of Italian. She spoke French imperfectly, mixed with German and Russian, in a subdued voice, rather hoarse. Her name was Xenia.

Old Balotta was very much put out. He thought that Mario should have married one of his old friend the advocate Bottiglia's daughters. And instead they now had with them this unknown woman, emerging from who knew what obscure life, who spoke French, a language which he and his wife did not know at all.

Balotta evinced a violent antipathy for Xenia, blind and unrestrainable. Vincenzino shared this antipathy with him. For the first time in all those years they were allies, Vincenzino and his father.

In the meanwhile Vincenzino, too, had married; and there was his wife, a clean, simple, honest woman of whom one knew everything, since her home was at Borgo Martino.

Mario and Xenia made a tour of the neighbourhood, looking for a house to buy. They went over a great number. Xenia would take a look with her large lack-lustre eyes. They were shadowed with bistre and the eyelids were heavy. She would whisper something in French and one would grasp that those houses were not to her liking.

In the end they bought the Villa Rondine, a large red suburban house, surrounded with shrubberies, lying on the top of the hill.

Balotta's children had known for a long time that they were rich, and they could see that with the years they were continually becoming more rich. Yet their habits did not change much. They always dressed in the same style and ate the same things. Signora Cecilia turned last winter's cloak at home herself with her maid Pinuccia's help. If she really wanted a new dress she called in Sestilia, the little village dressmaker.

Good fresh substantial food was always on the table at La Casetta and there was plenty of everything. But the tablecloth was rather worn after much laundering, and the glasses for every day were Cirio jam jars. The cover of the cheese dish had been broken and mended and Signora Cecilia was always saying—'I must buy another cheese dish.'

They kept two motor-cars at La Casetta, one a rather old heavy dark vehicle and the other a little one that could be opened, which Purillo used more than anyone else for going into town. They had many raincoats, many trunks and suitcases, many Scotch plaids and many pairs of skis. They had no hesitations about expenses for travelling, holidays, convalescences and doctors. But when Xenia arrived they realized that not one of them knew how to live expensively, and Xenia, on the other hand, did know.

They found that her clothes, always appearing somewhat crumpled and dusty, were, in fact, very expensive, and came from a famous dressmaking establishment in Paris. She had ordered these dresses, furs and shoes when they went to Paris after the wedding.

She installed herself at the Villa Rondine, furnishing the rooms with heavy and rather funereal pieces in a solemn style. She put up dark curtains on the windows, because she liked a dim light.

She engaged a number of menservants and maids with underlings of both sexes and was at a loss how to give orders to them all, speaking, as she did, only French and that with her wisp of a voice.

She sent to buy the meat at Cignano, where it was better but cost more. She sent the chauffeur to Castello to get the fruit early in the morning. She sent to Castel Piccolo for strawberries, to Soprano for cream cheese and to Torre for *grissini*.

She herself, however, ate very little, a lettuce leaf, a spoonful of broth. She had pineapples sent from the town, which she scarcely tasted, just a tiny mouthful on the tip of a fork.

She was, of course, thin, but imagined she was fat. She had installed a special heater in one of the bathrooms for vapour baths. She emerged from those baths more lean and emaciated than ever.

Her studio was in a large room on the ground floor. She would be there in black velvet trousers at her painting and sculpture, and moulding terracottas or pottery, which she then fired in a large kiln specially imported from Holland.

She never went down into the village. She went for walks in the garden, taking little steps and accompanied by her two pet dogs. They were curly-haired creatures of a grey tint verging on rose.

She never set foot in La Casetta. But at Christmas or Easter she sent everybody princely gifts.

In the evenings they were alone, she and Mario, in the great drawing-room crowded with dark pictures, valuable china and mirrors. A few candles in silver candelabra were lit, and there was no other light. They held each other's hands and played with the little dogs. Thus at times Purillo found them, the only person who ever went to Villa Rondine for an evening occasionally,

'With those candles,' said Signora Cecilia, 'they at any rate save on the electric light.'

That was not true, however; they paid enormous bills for electricity, too, probably because the kiln that had come from Holland was electric.

They bought a big black shiny motor-car which looked like a hearse. With her chauffeur, she went down to the town twice a week, buried in the back of the car, wearing dark glasses, her pale face sunk in the collar of her fur coat. She went there for the Turkish baths, because those vapour ones were no longer enough for her.

She had infected Purillo with the zest for spending. Purillo bought himself an Isotta-Fraschini. He bought himself a bed with a support for the back such as they have in nursing-homes, so as to be more comfortable when he read at night before going to sleep. Next to his room he installed a luxurious bathroom, with the bath set in the floor-level. A poky little hole, where in former days Magna Maria kept the hams hung up, had been converted for this.

When Xenia's first baby was due to arrive, Mario sent for a gynaecologist from Switzerland. The following year they had a baby again. They had a Swiss *nurse* with a blue veil. They had a Venetian nursemaid as well. Xenia fell ill after this and they removed her womb. She recovered and took up once more her sculpture, painting and walks with the pet dogs.

All her hair turned grey very early, and she never dyed it; one cannot say why.

Old Balotta, on the rare occasions on which he saw her, such as the children's birthdays, would say later to his wife,

'Did you see how old Xenia has become? Did you see how ugly she is? How can Mario bear to go to bed with her?'

Vincenzino explained everything by psychoanalysis.

He said that Mario had a mother-complex and felt protected by Xenia, who had an authoritarian temperament and ruled him and ordered him about.

Now and then old Balotta and Vincenzino revived their suspicions that she was a spy. Nothing was known about her, nothing of what she had done before she arrived in the neighbourhood. On the rare occasions when they met her, she spoke very little, and always in French, since she had never taken the trouble to learn Italian.

But Nebbia said,

'No, she is not a spy. She is merely a stupid woman, and so as not to let it be seen how stupid she is, she weaves all those mysteries about her. Like certain grubs which wrap themselves up in saliva so that no one gets at them.'

Mario meanwhile had become rather stout, went to bed early, and had had no more trouble with insomnia or fits of loquaciousness.

Vincenzino and his wife went to live at Casa Mercanti. It was a small house, immediately at the end of the village, and had a broad meadow in front of it in which were a few pear trees. Behind, it had a walled kitchen-garden full of cabbages.

Vincenzino's wife was called Catè. She was tall and sturdy. She had a wealth of blonde hair which she did sometimes in two tresses tightly pressed over the ears, and sometimes in a soft heavy mass, twisted and pinned on the crown of her head.

Her round face was bronzed with the sun and slightly freckled. She had high, prominent cheekbones and green eyes somewhat slanting upwards to her temples.

She was long remembered in the village returning from the stream where she went to bathe, with the wind catching up her short skirt over her shapely legs. Her hair would be damp and hang untidily over her forehead. Over her shoulder would be a wet towel soiled with sand.

People remembered her, too, coming down the hill, her mouth stained with mulberry juice, a tall handsome blonde with her blonde children.

When she went to the stream in summer she wore a blue dress with a white strip on the bottom of the skirt, and she tied up her hair in a handkerchief with blue and white spots. When she went ski-ing in winter she wore a white pull-over with the collar rolled back. On cool autumn evenings when she sat in the garden she had a black shawl over her shoulders, such as the poorer women wear.

She had married Vincenzino without love. But she had thought that he was so good, if a bit melancholy, and that he must therefore be intelligent.

She had also remembered that he had plenty of money and she had none.

Yet in those early days when she was at Casa Mercanti an infinite sadness came over her. She was there in the long afternoons looking at the cabbages in the garden behind the house. It seemed to her that the whole world was full of cabbages, and she used to cry because she longed so much to return to her mother.

Borgo Martino was not so far away, but she did not venture to go there, because her husband was against it.

At home in Borgo Martino was her mother, a widow, who owned a small stationery shop, and three small sisters who were at school. There was always a great deal of cheerfulness and noise in the house.

By contrast in Casa Mercanti silence always reigned. She went sometimes to the kitchen to pass the time discussing things with Pinuccia, the servant whom her mother-in-law Signora Cecilia had made over to her. She used to tell Pinuccia about her home, and the wild moments of laughter they had there, she and her sisters. Pinuccia listened as she peeled the potatoes and occasionally rubbed her nose with her chapped hand.

Late in the evening Vincenzino returned, and by then she had fallen asleep in her arm-chair waiting for him.

Vincenzino also had married without love. He had thought she was healthy, honest and a good girl.

He had also thought in some tortuous way that a marriage like that would please his father. For it could in some measure resemble Balotta's own marriage. He had chosen Cecilia from some neighbouring hamlet, choosing her because she was blonde, poor and healthy.

After he had married her Vincenzino realized that he had nothing to say to her. They passed the evenings in silence, the one opposite the other in arm-chairs in the sitting-room.

He read a book, picking his nose. Now and again he watched her knitting, her fair head leaning back in the rosy light of the lampshade. He thought her very beautiful, but did not consider that she was his type. He liked brunettes; blondes meant nothing to him.

In the afternoons, shut up in her room, she cried hard, by the window from which the cabbages could be seen. On coming home he found her with swollen face and reddened eyes. Then he gently asked her to go and see her mother the next day at Borgo Martino.

Little by little she got in the way of going there often, on her bicycle. She went almost every day. She also went sometimes on Sunday afternoon. On Sundays Vincenzino at any rate spent the afternoon sleeping, reading or studying plans for the factory and would not notice her going out.

Left alone in the house, Vincenzino went from room to room in his pyjamas. All the rooms were cool, dimly lit, and a restful silence reigned in them. Pinuccia had gone out, too. He poured himself out a large glass of whisky with ice and mineral water. He had learned to drink whisky in America. He settled into his arm-chair in the sitting-room with a book and the glass at his side.

He liked being alone in this way. He felt a profound relief and solace.

Then they had children. A boy was born and then a baby girl and then a boy again. In the meadow opposite the house nappies hung up to dry on a line fastened between two pear trees, and on the grass were toys and little pails to be seen. A country woman came from Soprano to look after the children, and she was provided with blue aprons. Catè was busy and had stopped crying. She did not go so often to Borgo Martino.

But she did not like anyone in the village. She found Signora Cecilia tiresome, an old *bergiana*, a word they used in her home at Borgo Martino. It meant something like a chatterbox. There was a coolness between her and Gemmina; there always had been, from the time when she had married Vincenzino. Possibly Gemmina was jealous of her for her good looks; or perhaps she thought she had married Vincenzino for his money, without love.

She did not take to Purillo. Xenia just seemed to her mad. She liked Nebbia well enough, especially because he came from Borgo Martino. But Pupazzina, Nebbia's wife, no, she did not care for her one little bit. She found her a bore, and thought she looked after her children badly. They were always rather dirty and never went out.

She used to go occasionally with Raffaella, Vincenzino's younger sister, to bathe in the stream. But she got bored with Raffaella, too. At eighteen Raffaella was more like a boisterous hobbledehoy. She let herself go playing with the children and she made them join in games that were too noisy and dangerous. She got them to dive into the whirlpools of the stream or climb up the highest rocks.

Catè embarked on spending money, seeing that there was so much of it. She ordered clothes for herself in the town, and also a cape of dark musquash. She did not wear it often, because it seemed to give her 'an air', as they used to say at home in Borgo Martino, 'like an old kangaroo'. This was a word which in their slang meant 'a madame.'

In imitation of Xenia she bought some tight trousers of black velvet. But Nebbia said they did not suit her, because they accentuated her hips.

She took offence at that and told Vincenzino that he could shut up, could Nebbia, and his wife, too, always dressed in ridiculous bits and pieces.

She got her *grissini* from Torre and sent Pinuccia to buy the strawberries at Castel Piccolo. Pinuccia would return, heated and sticky after coming up the path in the full sun, but without any strawberries, because they had already been all taken, early in the morning by those people at the Villa Rondine.

Occasionally she went to La Casetta to see Signora Cecilia. Cecilia showed her her hydrangeas, carnations and roses, and also a clump of moss-roses grown from seeds brought by Purillo from Holland.

Sometimes she went to Le Pietre. Barba Tommaso would meet her at the garden gate, and kiss her hand, brushing it lightly with his old cheek so rosy and well shaved. This was because he liked it to be said that he was still rather a roué, and that at seventy he could still pay court to the ladies.

Magna Maria was there, too, with her grey hair brushed back and her long red nose which had a wart on one nostril, the size of a pea, and she would offer her some apricots and a glass of sweet wine; she would embrace her and then embrace her again and keep saying,

'How are you? Are you well? Splendid, splendid! And the children? Splendid, splendid! And your mother? Splendid, splendid! But how splendid you are!'

She was not a bit amusing, all the same, that Magna Maria.

She got into the habit of going to the mountains every Sunday with Nebbia, Purillo and Raffaella for rock-climbing in the summer and ski-ing in the winter.

Raffaella behaved herself like a rowdy boy; she came down the slopes bawling like a wild thing and thumping everyone on the back with her hands heavy as lead. In the free air of the mountains she let herself go more than ever. She particularly delighted in playing tricks on Purillo, giving him soap when he asked for cheese, and cheese when he wanted soap. Or she put chestnut husks down his neck, which she had brought specially from the garden. Purillo patiently disentangled these husks from his woollen pullover. They were harmless tricks, rather stupid, learnt at school.

They all made fun of Purillo because he was such a Fascist, and they mimicked him receiving the Party officers at the works, and being lavish with the Roman salute.

Purillo would smile, arching his little mouth, pushing Raffaella's hand away as she gave him a punch in the stomach, heavy as lead.

Towards evening they stopped off at the rest house to have some mulled wine and sing,

Linda, Linda, my only true love,
You're cosy indoors, I've the heavens above!

It was Nebbia's song.

But Nebbia was always in a hurry to get home if he was not to find Pupazzina in a huff. Catè used to chaff him then for being afraid of Pupazzina.

They had left the car at Le Alpette, a little village on the road. It was always Nebbia's car, because Purillo—he and his Isotta-Fraschini—kept his in swaddling-clothes.

Catè used to find Vincenzino still sitting up, reading with his glass of whisky. She would try a little sip of it and make a grimace because she did not care about the strong flavour.

'How goes it, darling?' he said.

And he went on reading. She went to undress and chose a nightdress from the chest of drawers. She had a great many nightdresses; she liked pretty fine ones of embroidered silk, of *chiffon*.

'What a pretty nightdress!' Vincenzino said, coming in to undress.

She said,

'When I was a little girl my mother made me wear nightdresses of flowered flannel with long sleeves, which I could not bear.'

And she said as she was going to sleep,

'He is not so bad, after all, Purillo.'

For she was happy and felt full of tolerance and friendliness to everybody.

Then she began to go to parties and dances. Sometimes Vincenzino went with her; otherwise Purillo took her.

In the village they began saying that she was Purillo's lover. She knew that, because Pinuccia the maid reported it to her. She told Vincenzino, laughing.

'I and Purillo!'

But now when she came to La Casetta old Balotta looked at her sternly and found fault with everything she said.

Her two sisters sometimes came to Borgo Martino to look for her. They were as young as ever. They would stay the night and romp with the children, after supper. But she had an engagement for the evening and was dressing impatiently.

Vincenzino would say to her,

'Why don't you take your sisters with you as well?'

She would say as she was putting on her earrings,

'No, they are too young. And anyhow they have not been asked.'

The truth was she did not want to take them with her for fear that people would find them rather common.

She said,

'And they haven't anything to wear either.'

Vincenzino said,

'Tomorrow you can buy them some clothes.'

Sometimes Nebbia came to spend the evening with them. He left Pupazzina at home because Catè and she could not bear one another. Nebbia discussed things about the works with Vincenzino, and they two were in agreement against old Balotta, whose ideas were old-fashioned.

She got bored and waited for the conversation to turn on something nice.

She said,

'How tiresome you are!'

'Be quiet for a bit, dear,' Nebbia would say to her.

They used familiar terms to each other because they had been friends from childhood.

'Life,' she said one evening to Nebbia, 'is really fine.'

She had enjoyed herself very much in the afternoon at a tea given at the Villa Rondine. She had met a violinist, a friend of Xenia, who was staying at the time at the Villa Rondine; a little fellow whom everyone there called *maestro* except Xenia, who was more familiar with him.

'Life,' said Nebbia, 'is fine for me and for Vincenzino because we have things to do. But for you it must be an awful bore, because you do nothing all day long.'

'I? I do nothing?' said she.

'Well no. What do you do?' said Nebbia.

'And your wife? Your wife, what does she do?' said she.

'My wife,' said Nebbia, 'does not do anything either. You have the servants for the children and the house. You are bourgeoisie and get bored like every fine lady.'

'I am not a fine lady I am not bourgeois! I do not know why, but I am not bourgeois, not even in my dreams.'

Vincenzino began to laugh.

'Anyhow,' said she, 'even if I am *bourgeois*, it is nothing to me. And I am not bored, because I enjoy myself. And even if I have a nursery maid, I am busy with the children, and take them out in any sort of weather. Pupazzina, on the other hand, never takes hers out for fear of their catching cold. Look how pale they are. And mine never have sore throats.'

She had spoken rapidly and remained breathless. But Nebbia would not have anything said about his Pupazzina.

He said, 'Leave Pupazzina alone. What has she done to you?'

'Nothing to me,' she said and shrugged her shoulders.

And then she said, 'I have been at the Villa Rondine today. They have now set up two big angels, of gilded wood, in the hall. They found them in an antique shop, in the town. They are not a bit pretty.

'We shall have to move house,' she said. "We are cramped here. We have not even got an ironing-room, and the ironing has to be done in the kitchen. At the Villa Rondine they have a large ironing-room, complete with fitted cupboards, and the linen well arranged. And now they have renovated the kitchen, with a marble floor; it is lovely.'

'I am not even thinking of moving house,' said Vincenzino. 'I am quite all right here.'

They had this argument about the house almost every evening.

'Xenia,' said she, 'is not at all unlikeable. She is always very nice to me.'

Meanwhile Nebbia, as not being interested in these discussions, had fallen asleep, with his head on the back of the arm-chair, and was smiling faintly in his sleep.

'Why does he come here, if he goes to sleep?' said Catè. 'He has become awfully boring, has Nebbia. He is a perfect fool.'

After Nebbia had gone away they began to get ready for bed; meanwhile Vincenzino was still wandering round the rooms, and would pick up a book and plunge his nose in it.

She was thinking about that violinist whom she had met at Xenia's; and of how he had remained sitting by her side on a stool, and had told her that she had such an interesting head and resembled Botticelli's *Primavera.*

His name was Giorgio Tebaldi. He was a very little man with grey hair, and a rather sing-song voice, just slightly so.

He was so small that he did not come up to her shoulder, and already entirely grey, and not at all young, he could not be.

She did not care about him; and yet had been content to stay there for an eternity, in the drawing-room at the Villa Rondine, listening to that gentle singing voice which soothed her.

That voice seemed to stir plaintively within her if she thought about it again; a kind of plaintive sound which annoyed her, and yet stirred her.

'How lovely it is, how lovely to be alive! and how dangerous! It is really dangerous, but so lovely.' Those were her thoughts.

'I am not bourgeois at all,' she said to Vincenzino, who had undressed beside her. 'Nebbia understands nothing. His wife, yes; she is a true bourgeois. But I, no.'

'No, darling,' said Vincenzino.

And they fell asleep.

The next day Xenia sent to invite her up to the Villa Rondine again. They were in the garden, Xenia and the violinist, drinking grapefruit juice in green glasses.

Because of Xenia it was necessary to speak French. Catè got on badly in French and was ashamed of it.

Then they went into the drawing-room and Xenia sat down to the piano. He put a handkerchief on his shoulder, set his chin on the violin, tightened the muscles of his face and played Sibelius's *Valse Triste*. Xenia accompanied him at the piano with a dreamy ironic look in her large eyes, so heavily shadowed, and hummed the music with closed lips.

Then the three of them went for a stroll in the shrubbery, with the little dogs ahead of them.

The day after, he came for her and the two of them went alone to the town to the antique dealer, because she had said that she liked those gilded angels, and would like similar ones.

But it was not true that she liked them, and she had only said so to be polite to Xenia, and because she was feeling happy.

The dealer had not got any more of those angels, but there was instead a Moor's head, and he told her that it was very fine.

She bought it.

The dealer undertook to send it to her. Then they went on to a café. The café was very dark and deserted, and they sat down in a corner, right at the back. He gazed at her. She did not know what to say and was twisting her scarf in her hands.

She felt she was snared under his gaze, as though in the meshes of a net. She was uneasy, and had a great desire to run away, and at the same time to remain there.

He said with that caressing voice,

'It is lovely for me to have met you, dear.'

She said, in a stupid way,

'You simply must not be so familiar.'

Immediately she felt ashamed of having spoken so. She looked at the clock and said it was time for the motor-bus, and she must be going.

As the bus was full, only she was able to sit down, and he remained standing near the ticket-desk.

She watched him, being some way from him. So small, with his grey hair, a light soft hat, too big for him, a hand in his pocket, and an absorbed rather sad look.

Then she thought that all men, if one observed them rather closely, had that air of being unprotected, solitary and absorbed, and that troubled a woman: and she thought that that was very dangerous.

She asked him to come in for a moment and have some tea.

Vincenzino came in while they were having tea in

the sitting-room. As always happened when someone was introduced to him, Vincenzino threw back his shoulders, and had that sharp look of his, like a cold flash of light.

He sat down and talked about music, gazing into space: a long interminable murmur. After a little while Giorgio Tebaldi went away.

She went to her room, and threw herself on the bed; she had a great impulse to laugh and at the same time was frightened.

'How small he is, how small! Tiny!' she said and laughed all by herself. 'And he is not a bit good-looking, he is ugly. Vincenzino is better and even Nebbia and Purillo.'

She could see him as he put the handkerchief on his shoulder, rested his chin on his violin and tightened the muscles of his face: and now she did not know why, but he worried her with that violin and the handkerchief.

Just once she had called him *maestro* and had felt very ridiculous, because she was not used to addressing people so.

The next day the Moor's head arrived: and she put it in the sitting-room on a bookcase. Vincenzino found it very ugly; and Nebbia thought it horrible. But Vincenzino told her to keep it there all the same in the sitting-room, if she liked it.

He did not care a bit about ornaments and decorations.

The next day Giorgio Tebaldi again called for her, and they went for a walk in the country.

So, they became lovers.

It lasted for a few days; and then he went away. He sent her two postcards, one from Verona, and one from Florence, just with his signature only. He had asked her if she could write to him sometimes, to a poste-restante: but she had said no.

'It has been nothing, nothing,' she reflected. 'It happens to so many women, to so many it happens, it is nothing, no one has known of it, and I must go on as if it had never happened.'

But she was sick of the Moor's head, and put it in the shoe-cupboard. Moreover, she found it rather distasteful to go back to the Villa Rondine. However, she went back there sometimes, because now Xenia often gave tea parties and at-homes. It seemed to her that there was a vaguely ironic smile in her heavy weary eyes, as she handed some fruit juice in a green glass, just as on that day a while ago.

One evening while they were coming home from the Villa Rondine she said to Vincenzino,

'You know, I was a bit in love with that violinist.'

'What violinist?' he said.

'Giorgio Tebaldi.'

'Ah.'

After a long silence he asked,

'Did you make love?'

'No,' she said. 'No.'

But her heart was as heavy as stone, for having lied.

At times she began to cry, when she was alone, and said,

'Oh, why am I so unfortunate?'

And she said, 'If Vincenzino was not so strange, if he would talk to me, if only he were different! If he were different, more like other people! Then I should be a different woman, much better!'

After that she began to make love with those who came her way; she even made love with Purillo. With Nebbia, no, she never made love with him, because it never entered her head to do so with Nebbia; he was tied to Pupazzina.

Vincenzino knew everything, and she saw well enough that he knew everything; she hated him, because he knew, and nevertheless continued to be the same as ever, to go for walks by himself, to drink whisky, to write up plans for the works, and to read books, plunging his nose into them.

5

Vincenzino and Catè

AFTER the war Vincenzino and Catè separated. The children were in Rome, at school.

Through the whole period of the war Catè and Xenia with their children had been at Sorrento. Sorrento had been Xenia's idea, a happy idea because, in fact, the fighting did not pass that way.

Later Catè and Xenia quarrelled, over a matter of linen. But it was an excuse, as their relations had deteriorated for some time through inscrutable reasons.

Catè went away from Sorrento and took a house in Rome in the Viale Parioli.

Mario returned from being a prisoner in Germany with his lungs in a bad state and with some internal trouble. He and Xenia went back to the Villa Rondine. Xenia had a homoeopathic doctor brought from Switzerland, and installed him permanently in the house, to look after Mario.

This doctor treated him with minute doses of a green powder, and then with certain white pills, and ordered him a diet of raw vegetables which Xenia mixed in an electric shredder, a thing that had just come into fashion and was called a Gogo.

Mario was happy.

All the same, he died in a few months, always happy and full of confidence in the doctor, with whom he played chess all day long. In these last days the doctor, being scared, had him moved to a clinic in the town, where he died.

Xenia left the Villa Rondine, and Purillo came to live there. Xenia established herself in the town with her children and married the Swiss doctor, continuing, however, always to wear a widow's black clothes, and to have dozens and dozens of eggs sent in from the country, since those of the town did not seem any too fresh.

Raffaella, who had joined the partisans, did not manage to accustom herself to a quiet way of life again. She enrolled in the Communist Party, and toured the countryside on a bicycle with propaganda booklets. Tommasino was at school at Salice and came home when he had finished there, a tall thin youth of eighteen.

Tommasino and Raffaella went to live together in a small apartment in the heart of the village, behind the works. They had their meals in the restaurant at the Concordia. But Purillo told them they could build themselves a good house.

Raffaella did not want to and said that the money was not theirs at all, but belonged to the workers.

However, Raffaella and Tommasino did have a house built. A very modern house, quite circular, with a flat roof and an outside spiral staircase. It stands above the Villa Rondine on the brow of the hill.

Raffaella bought a horse. She had had a mania for horses from childhood.

Tommasino enrolled in the Agricultural Society and lived in the town. He came to the country on Saturdays. Raffaella had left the Communist Party, and had joined a little group of dissident Communists which had only three members in the whole district.

In contrast Vincenzino belonged to the Christian Left.

Vincenzino had served in the war on the Greek front, had been taken prisoner and sent to India. He returned to Italy more than a year after the end of the war. Catè and the children were in Rome.

They sent the children to boarding school. By now they were youngsters. Both Catè and Vincenzino were in agreement not to remain together.

Catè had now had her hair cut and wore it very short and brushed back. She had developed a thin hard face with the mouth somewhat drawn down.

As for Vincenzino, he was always just the same.

Only, he wore spectacles now for reading, having become long-sighted.

They came back to the village together. Catè stopped at the Concordia, and he went to sleep at Casa Mercanti. They did not consider themselves now husband and wife any longer. They were very polite to one another; but every now and then quarrels broke out between them on the slightest pretext.

Raffaella came to the Concordia to look for Catè.

Catè wished to go to the cemetery to take some flowers for Balotta and Signora Cecilia. They went, she and Raffaella. Balotta and his wife were buried together in a tomb with a dome, like a small villa, surrounded by little trees. Balotta had bought the tomb a long time ago when he fell ill with trouble in his gall bladder.

Catè cried, blowing her nose loudly in a tiny handkerchief. Her mother had died, too, during the war at Borgo Martino. Her sisters had married and gone to live elsewhere. The stationery shop had vanished, a garage having been put in its place.

They went on to Le Pietre. There was Barba Tommaso still, as always, fresh, rosy, handsome, but in his second childhood. He did not recognize Catè and asked Raffaella in a loud voice,

'Who is it, who is it?'

Magna Maria was in the kitchen with the maid Pinuccia, whom they now had.

Pinuccia and Catè kissed.

Magna Maria gave her some sweet wine and figs, and said,

'So, you have cut your hair off. Ah, splendid, splendid!'

She said it, however, with less assurance than of old.

As they came away Catè asked Raffaella to show her the place behind Le Pietre where they had murdered Nebbia.

They went. There was a large tall pointed rock stained with lichen. It was just there that they had murdered him.

Catè cried. She touched everything, the rock, the trees around it and the clump of bushes where they found his hat. She looked and touched and wept.

She had not wanted to see Gemmina or Purillo. So they came back by the roadway, avoiding going by La Casetta, and passed by the shrubbery of the Villa Rondine.

Catè continued to cry. Raffaella said,

'How you cry! You are a regular fountain!'

However, she took her to her house, and made her lie down on a bed, and gave her a hot-water bottle and some aspirin.

Catè said,

'Why is everything ruined, everything?'

'What is ruined?' said Raffaella.

She wanted to take her to the stables to see the horse before she went away. But Catè knew little about horses. However, she looked at it and smiled, being anxious to please, and said its coat was a good colour. She touched its tail with one finger. But the horse started, and kicked, and she was frightened.

'You have always been a great coward,' said Raffaella. 'Do you remember when we went to the mountains and your legs were all of a tremble coming down, and Nebbia got cross?'

'Yes,' said Catè.

'And when we went to the stream with the children, and I wanted us to dive, and you were afraid?'

'Yes,' said Catè and began to cry once more.

'That's enough, for God's sake,' said Raffaella.

Meanwhile Vincenzino had come for her, so she washed her face and said good-bye to Raffaella and went off with Vincenzino by the path which leads to Casa Mercanti.

'What a hideous place!' said Catè. 'What a hideous, hideous place! A really stupid place! I don't know how I managed to stay here all those years.'

They had to make an inventory of the furniture, empty the cupboards, count the articles that belonged to the one or the other, count the plates and table things.

Vincenzino put on his spectacles and began to write in a pocket-book.

Catè, kneeling on the carpet, set about counting the spoons and forks.

'I don't care a rap about all these spoons,' she said suddenly.

'I care less about them than you do,' he said.

'Then why do we count them?'

'Because it is the thing to do,' said he.

She sighed and began again.

'What will you do with this house?' she said. 'Will you come and live here with someone?'

'I don't know,' said he.

'It is a fine house,' she said, 'and yet I did not like it when I was here and wanted to look for another, and you did not want to. Do you remember?'

'Yes.'

'I was foolish,' she said. 'I was foolish, just because I was young, nothing else.

'I got depressed,' she said, 'looking at all those cabbages from the windows of our room. Now there are no more cabbages on that piece of land. Have they begun to build a shop or something?

'And there, sitting in that arm-chair of an evening,' she said, 'used to be Nebbia, and it was all so nice, and it seemed nothing to have him sitting there, asleep, and now we shall never see him any more!'

'Happiness,' he said, 'always seems nothing. It is like water; one only realizes it when it has run away.'

'That is true,' she said. She thought for a moment and said,

'It is the same with the evil we do; it seems nothing, just seems foolishness, cold water, while we are doing it. Otherwise people would not do it; they would be more careful.'

'True,' he said.

She said, 'Why have we ruined everything, everything?' and she began to cry. She said,

'I can't leave this house. I brought up my children here. I have been here so many years, so many years. I can't—I can't leave it.'

'Then you want to stay here?' he asked.

And she said, 'No'—and went away the next day.

Vincenzino remained alone.

For a while he stayed at Casa Mercanti, then he moved to the house where Raffaella and Tommasino were, on the brow of the hill.

He went to Rome, once or twice a month, to see his children. Catè was there in Rome, in her apartment in the Viale Parioli. They never saw one another.

He used to take the children sweets and presents. He also took them on one occasion a flute. But they were not interested in music; they only liked mechanical things, motors.

The Christian Left was disbanded and he did not belong to any party after that. He wrote a book about his time as a prisoner in India, and had a resounding success with it.

He was surprised, and pleased also; then he immediately put it out of his thoughts.

He was now in sole command at the works. His hands were free, and he was able to do as he pleased. He had many plans in his head and he was able to realize them. There was a whole world of things in his head.

He was always the same, with his fair curly hair thick and close like a carpet. He hadn't a grey hair. He had developed a cool rather weary manner of authority that appealed to the women.

He could probably have had all the women he wanted. But he did not want anyone.

When he went to the town he ended up occasionally by spending the evening at Xenia's. He played chess with the Swiss doctor whom Xenia had married, and drank whisky. The doctor gave him advice about his liver, which he had ruined with whisky, and prescribed some minute doses of that green powder of his in little papers.

In the village he sometimes spent the evenings with

Purillo. It surprised him that he liked passing the time in this way, with his old enemies, Xenia and Purillo.

Purillo was still very much scared, when he returned from Switzerland after the war, so scared that before he did return he had waited some time and could not make up his mind. To begin with he remained shut up in the Villa Rondine without ever setting foot in the works. He was thin, wasted away by fear, and there he was in the house with his *purillo* cap on his head and wearing an overcoat because there at the Villa Rondine the water was frozen in the central-heating system and the boilers had burst: they had to burn wood in the stoves, which did not draw and heated badly.

He was assailed with regrets for having been a Fascist. That seemed to him an enormous act of folly, quite unforgivable, which had put a stain on his whole life. At times he spoke of making away with himself. Vincenzino had to comfort him and calm him down.

He begged Vincenzino to tell everybody that he, Purillo, had saved Balotta, by taking him away from the village. The Fascists would have killed old Balotta if he had not taken him to Cignano.

'But they know that in the village,' said Vincenzino, and looked at him sitting there with his *purillo* cap, his badly shaved cheeks, his Adam's apple protruding from his unfastened collar, and his pale hands with folds of skin on their backs. He had hated him so much, he had wasted so much hate on that moustache, that turned-up nose—yes, he had wasted so much hatred, and so much fear also, fear that he might take the factory from him, and the power and his father's affection, and who knows what else. And now of all that great hatred there remained nothing at all any more, and even that was saddening.

Raffaella was always coming to see Purillo. She relit the stoves which had gone out, and asked his advice about the horse. Purillo told her that he knew about horses, having had a friend in his youth who owned some stables.

He told Raffaella that he wished to kill himself, since he had blundered so badly and his life made no sense any more.

Raffaella said,

'But are you mad? You would not seriously want to kill yourself! Put that right out of your head!'

She thumped him on the back with hands heavy as lead, and said,

'You were not the only Fascist. Italy was full of them!'

Then she said,

'Come and join my party.'

Purillo said,

'Communist, I? Never!'

'But you don't know that I am not a Communist any longer?' said Raffaella. 'I am a Trotzkyite. For Trotzky. . . . But bless me you don't know who Trotzky was anyhow.'

Little by little Purillo's spirit revived. He returned to work at the factory. He also began to see something of people again, the Sartorios, the Terenzis, the Bottiglias.

He would not join any party. He said that politics made him feel sick. Nevertheless, sometimes of an evening at General Sartorio's he nerved himself to say,

'All the same, Mussolini was the right man.'

And he stuck his thumbs in his waistcoat.

'A pity,' he said, 'he sided with the Germans. If he had not sided with the Germans, things would have gone very differently. If only Italy, like Switzerland, had remained neutral.'

He took to talking about Switzerland, where he had been so long, and which he said he knew like the seat of his trousers.

He began going round the dairy-farms again as he did before the war, on one excuse or another, and made love to all the peasant women. In the village he had the reputation of being a Don Juan.

In the village, when they see a peasant girl with a baby in her arms, they say,

'That's one of Purillo's.'

They credit him with hundreds of children.

Then the rumour began to go round that he was marrying Raffaella. People were staggered.

'Poor thing,' they said. 'Raffaella, poor thing! What a tragedy, what a tragedy!'

Vincenzino learned of it from Gemmina. He, too, was staggered. Then he was overcome by rage and could have smashed everything before him.

Vincenzino and Raffaella were living in the same house. They used to have dinner and supper together. Yet she had not told him anything.

'Purillo,' said Gemmina, 'must have brooded over and calculated over this for some time. Perhaps even when Mama and Papa were alive.'

She said, 'It is a good thing that Balotta is not here to see this.' She had a way of calling her father Balotta at times, and she added,

'Purillo is like a snake which has long sight.'

'I never knew that snakes had long sight,' said Tommasino, who was also present.

That evening Vincenzino said to Raffaella,

'Is it true that you are marrying Purillo?'

'Yes,' said she.

Now that he had her before his eyes, he no longer felt angry. He was only very uneasy and put out.

He said, 'But why?'

She said, 'Because I am in love with him.'

He reflected that when he married Catè he was not in love with her; on the contrary, he had some strange theories in his head. He remained silent.

But all that night in bed he tossed about between the sheets and said, 'But how can one be in love with Purillo.'

He gave himself no peace over it, and even asked Tommasino first thing in the morning, while he was shaving in the bathroom,

'How can one be in love with Purillo?'

Tommasino did not know either.

Gradually he ceased to think about it. Why vex oneself over other people? Everyone did as he thought best.

He gave Raffaella a refrigerator for a wedding present. They were beginning to come into fashion. But no one in the village so far had had one.

Raffaella went to live at the Villa Rondine. She wanted to take the horse with her; but Purillo forebade it. Where were they to put it at the Villa Rondine? There was no stall there.

So the horse stayed on at Casa Tonda; that is what Raffaella called the house on the brow of the hill.

It remained there for a while, and was groomed by the peasant woman's sons. To begin with Raffaella came almost every day to see it. Then she forgot about it.

Finally they sold it.

Raffaella and Purillo had a baby which was called Pepè.

Raffaella as a mother proved a great coward. She carried Pepè bundled up in wool and she did nothing but put on and take off his pullovers and shorts. She never dreamed of plunging him in the icy waters of the stream as she had done with Catè and Vincenzino's children, all that long time ago.

Vincenzino and Tommasino talked occasionally when alone. Vincenzino had taken a fancy to his younger brother. He told him things that he had never mentioned to anyone. He would begin usually in the evening, after supper. He gazed into space and began to speak with that long slow murmur.

Sometimes he spoke of Catè. He had a strange notion of their relations.

He spoke of the day when as a little child still he had seen Purillo kill a dog by stoning it.

Purillo did not like animals, one had always known that. That was why he had not wanted the horse.

According to Vincenzino, the strong impression which had been made on him as a child when the dog was stoned had bred in his soul a great horror of cruelty.

Through this horror of cruelty he had given Catè the freedom to detach herself from him, by not exercising any force on her, in order that she should not be wounded and suffer.

And so he had lost her.

Tommasino was not much convinced by such a complicated chain of thought. But he agreed, because Vincenzino did not at all like being contradicted once he had got an idea in his head.

Vincenzino said that he had many times regretted what he had done to Catè. He realized well enough that without intending it he had wounded her and made her suffer.

And so often her voice echoed in his memory when she said,

'Oh, why, why have we ruined everything?'

Many a time at night he could not sleep and could hear her lamenting in that way.

They talked until a late hour, and drank whisky. Then they went to bed. In his room on the top floor Vincenzino lay in a bed with a support so that he could read sitting up before going to sleep. He had copied it from Purillo.

Vincenzino now knew a good many people in the town. But in his heart he liked to be with Tommasino—that was enough; or at most with some others of his family, with Raffaella and Gemmina, or even with Magna Maria.

This was perhaps because these had known Catè;

all the other people in the town had never known her.

He set about writing another book, and had a number of plans and ideas.

He had an accident with his motor-car, while he was on his way to Rome to see his children. He was alone. It was beginning to get dark and it was raining. The car skidded on the asphalt.

Some peasants found him soon afterwards, flung across the steering wheel, and they summoned a motor-ambulance.

He died in hospital. Purillo was telephoned for and got there in time to be with him at the last. But Tommasino—no, he did not make it in time.

6

Elsa and Tommasino

TOMMASINO eats by himself with a book propped against his glass. Betta, the peasant woman, comes to summon him to meals.

Betta comes and goes to and from the kitchen; she is squat, broad and fat, wearing a cambric dress with white spots.

Betta says,

'Did you like the steak, Tommasino?'

Betta addresses him familiarly, having known him as a child.

'And tomorrow,' she says, 'as there is some of the beef left, I will cut it up in small pieces and do it ever so slowly with onion.'

She says, 'Now I'll finish the dishes, and then sweep and then wash out those two cloths. Then I'll put the beans to soak, so that tomorrow, when I come, I can put them on to cook with a little parsley, garlic and meat, eh?'

Tommasino sits down in the arm-chair with his book near the light.

'Alone like this, poor dear,' says Betta. 'You should find yourself a beautiful wife. You are rich, you are good-looking, you are young, and here in the village there are plenty of good girls, rich and pretty, who are waiting for you.'

She says, 'Do you want me to bring you that thingummy, Tommasino?'

The thingummy is a tape-recorder. When Tommasino is alone there in the evening, he talks into the recorder if any ideas come to him.

Then he takes it to bed with him, because when he is in bed and about to go to sleep still more ideas come to him.

The dining-room at the Casa Tonda is a big one with large windows, and almost empty, because nobody has ever thought of putting settees or pictures there.

'I,' says Betta, 'If I was rich as you, I would put a side-table there with shelves above it up on that wall. As it is, it's awkward with the plates, and I have to go to the kitchen for them.'

From the windows one sees the hillside all bare, then the trees of the Villa Rondine, the village, the lights of Castello and Castel Piccolo, the night sky.

Says Betta, 'A lad like you should never be alone. A lad like you, so rich, should have friends and girls, always something going on.'

She says, 'If I had all that money, I wouldn't stay here. I should always be going about and enjoying the world—travelling. I should never stay still, I should always be travelling.'

She says, 'Purillo has just diddled you out of the factory.'

She says, 'The money, you have that, but as for managing, he manages, and when Vincenzino's children arrive here, grown up, they will get nothing, because it will all be Pepè's.'

She says, 'But that is just of no concern to you; you haven't the itch for it, and at the end of the month you get your money all the same.'

She says, 'You are a nice kind gentleman, and you haven't the guts to fight against Purillo.'

She says, 'Now I am going home. I shall sit by the stove, and remake a dress. It is a brown dress, old; it is not so ugly, but I do not like it any more, so I thought like this. I am unstitching it, as Magna Maria has given me some red silk, not very much, all small pieces. With these small pieces I am entirely remaking the sleeves with the cuffs and the collar.'

'A happy thought,' says Tommasino.

'Then the buttons—I have bought the hearts, and am taking them to Cignano to have them covered.'

'You have bought the hearts?'

'Those black little balls, for buttons.'

'Ah.'

'The collar—I am making it round, *à la Carletta.*'

'Good.'

'Well, good night, *ciao*, Tommasino!'

'Ciao!'

Tommasino remains there, and twists his hair round his fingers. Then he sweeps his hair back, goes to his typewriter, and taps out some words.

Then he gets up, slips on his overcoat, leaves the house and goes down the hill. He has an old overcoat, too short and worn at the cuffs, with the pockets out of shape. Gemmina for some time has said that he ought to get a new one made for him.

He keeps his motor-car in the Concordia garage. The car cannot get up as far as Casa Tonda.

At the bar of the Concordia he has a Martini with quinine, because there is not much choice there.

He gets in his motor-car and goes to the cinema at Cignano.

They are doing *Fiery Darkness.*

He stays at the back of the almost empty room with a cigarette, his coat collar turned up and his hands in his pockets.

He has a Bisler at the bar in Cignano.

Everyone knows him and greets him. He responds by bringing his hand to his forehead, in a sort of flabby military salute. It is a salute which he has kept up since his schooldays.

He returns home, gets into his pyjamas, wanders barefoot round the kitchen, looks inside a saucepan where the beans are soaking.

Then he sits down on his bed with his typewriter on his knees and taps out a few words.

Then he scratches his head hard, yawns, wrinkles his nose and gets under the bed-clothes.

He has his tape-recorder on the bedside table. He says something, then listens to his own voice, which babbles undecidedly in the recorder, an extraneous and lamentable presence in the empty house.

He thrusts his head under the pillow, turns the light out and sleeps.

Tommasino spends almost all his evenings like that, or he goes to the Villa Rondine, or sometimes to parties and dances with the girls, if it is a waltz.

He does not know any other dances. Only the waltz.

At the Villa Rondine he annoyed Raffaella—because he showed his dislike of Pepè.

The Villa Rondine has not much changed since the days of Xenia and Mario. On leaving the house Xenia had taken all the furniture, but Purillo had bought similar things to replace them. Purillo having, as Vincenzino always said, no personality of his own.

Purillo sits there with Borzaghi in a corner of the sitting-room—they play chess.

Purillo asks Tommasino,

'How are your researches getting on on linear programming?'

Raffaella asks, 'This linear programming! What is it?'

'Linear programming is a sort of line which goes straight from production to consumer. Straight.'

Tommasino explains this, blushing, because Borzaghi is there and he would enjoy having Borzaghi listening.

He explains, with the help of the gestures of his long white thin fingers, and blushing a little because linear programming is dear to him, and he feels shy about talking aloud about it thus.

Raffaella says, 'I don't understand a single word of it', and she adds, 'Tommasino, why don't you join my party?'

Her party is that of the dissident Communists, as always. It is seldom in her thoughts now, and she only remembers it occasionally, principally to annoy Purillo. Communists, dissident or not, give him a stomach-ache. She thinks little about it, because nowadays her only thoughts are for Pepè.

Raffaella says,

'You, Tommasino, are no doubt very intelligent.

What a pity you are so unsettled. Why don't you marry?'

'I don't want that!' said Tommasino.

'He is married to linear programming,' said Purillo, and he winks at Borzaghi, who smiles in agreement.

Tommasino goes practically every day to the works. Sometimes he finds nothing to do there. He has a fine room, a fine table, a telephone with lots of red and green buttons, and a revolving armchair on which every so often he takes a half-spin.

He has a large morocco writing-pad well furnished with blotting-paper, a pen placed upright in a stand, a block for notes, and a pencil on a chain.

He doodles with his pen on the blotting-paper, and writes on the block—

'Heart of buttons. Little black ball.'

And then he leans his head on the table, presses his eyelids with his thumbs, and thinks of linear programming, a line which goes straight from producer to consumer, straight.

Tommasino and I met every Wednesday in the town.

He waited for me outside the 'Selecta' library. There he would be in his old overcoat, a bit shabby, his hands in his pockets, leaning against the wall.

He would greet me, bringing his hand to his forehead and taking it away, with a languid smartness.

We only saw one another in the town. We avoided meeting in the village. He wished it so.

For months and months we had been meeting in this way, on Wednesdays, often on Saturdays as well, and we always did the same things; we changed the book at the 'Selecta' library, bought some oat-cakes, bought also for my mother fifteen centimetres of black gros-grain.

Then we went to a room which he had hired in the Via Gorizia, on the top floor.

The room had a round table in the middle covered with a piece of carpet, and on the table was a glass cloche which protected some branches of coral. There was also a little stove behind a curtain where we could make coffee, if we wanted to.

He said to me sometimes,

'See, I am not marrying you', and I would laugh and say, 'I know that.'

He said, 'I don't want to marry; if I did, I should probably marry you.'

And he would add, 'Is that enough for you?' and I would say, 'I can make it do.'

Those were the words of our servant Antonia when my mother asked her if she had enough cheese.

'And the linear programming?' I said.

'Thanks,' said he, 'that's all right.'

He remained stretched out with his hands clasped

under his head, with his thin fine countenance, and his serious mouth. Sometimes he would ask me,

'And you?'

'I, what?'

'And you? And the little Bottiglia girls?'

We would return to the village on the last bus, the one at ten o'clock in the evening.

He always sat at a distance from me, at the back, with his coat-collar turned up, and gazed out of the window.

We got out in the piazza, opposite the Hotel Concordia and he saluted me in his usual way, and we made off in opposite directions, he up a steep lane that goes to Casa Tonda, and I by the path which skirts General Sartorio's wood.

I ate a little supper in the kitchen and my mother looked on.

She would say, 'Today I have been well all along, though towards evening I felt a sort of cold void in my stomach, and I had to eat a biscuit.'

She said, 'Have you brought the oat-cakes?'

When my mother reckoned up in her thoughts the men in the village whom I might marry she never lingered over Tommasino.

Perhaps she thought him too rich; somewhat out of our reach. And then she found him odd, going about dressed like a pauper, and always pale; he must have bad health.

She said that all Balotta's children, for one thing or another, dead or alive, had always had eccentric ideas and had brought trouble on themselves.

When my mother watched me while I ate my supper in the kitchen, how remote was any suspicion that only a few hours before Tommasino and I had been together on the top floor in the Via Gorizia.

My mother does not even know that the Via Gorizia exists; she hardly ever goes down to the town.

Aunt Ottavia says to her,

'Why don't we go to the town sometimes?'

And my mother says, 'What for?'

Sometimes Tommasino was in a black mood and would not talk.

I used to suggest a walk then, and we walked interminably, in silence, in the park, along the river.

We would sit down on a bench; behind us in the middle of the park was the castle with its red turrets and spires and the drawbridge: and on the side there was the glassed-in veranda of the restaurant, deserted at that hour: two waiters would be there expectantly all the same, among the tables, with napkins under their arms.

There was the silent river in front of us, with its

green waters, and the boats moored to the bank, the shelter of the landing-stage built on piles, the wooden steps against which the waves lapped.

He would stroke my face and say, 'Poor Elsa.'

'Why poor?' I said. 'Why do you think me that?'

'Because you have fallen in with me who am a disaster.'

'Yet,' I would say, 'you have always got the linear programming.'

'That, yes, I have always got that,' he said and laughed.

We walked interminably by the river. He looked about him and said. 'But this is quite country. We come to the town, and then we always go to look for the country, is it not so?'

I said to him, 'It is because we pretend not to know each other when we are in the village.'

He said, 'Because we are queer.'

He said, 'It is for your reputation. I must not compromise you, seeing that I am not going to marry you.'

I laughed and said, 'My reputation! I don't care a rap for that, not I.'

He twisted his hair round his fingers, and stopped for a moment to think.

'In the village,' he said, 'I don't feel free. Everything weighs on me.'

'What weighs on you?'

'Everything weighs on me,' he said, 'everything—Purillo, the factory, Gemmina, and even the dead. Even the dead—do you understand?—weigh on me.

'Some day or other,' he said, 'I shall pack it up and go away.'

And I would say to him, 'And not take me with you?'

'I should think, no.'

We walked a little in silence.

'You,' he said to me, 'ought to find someone to marry you. Not immediately, of course, but in a little while.'

He said, 'You haven't any need at all to marry immediately. What hurry is there?

'And you are quite all right,' he said, 'with me, like this.'

'With you, like this, Wednesdays and Saturdays?' I said.

'Yes, like this, no?'

'We must go back now,' I said. 'It will soon be time for the bus.'

We turned, retraced our steps through the park, skirted the castle walls, and crossed the bridge which shook under the wheels of the trams.

'I don't say it is ideal for you, like this,' he said.

'And for you?' I said to him. 'Is it ideal for you?'

'Oh,' he said, 'I am without ideals.'

I laughed and said to him, 'Poor Tommasino.'

'Why poor, when I have all that money?'

It was morning, and I had only just got up and was standing on the balcony. I saw Signora Bottiglia, who had got a hoe and was hoeing the flower bed.

'Hullo!' she called. *'Ciao!'*

Signora Bottiglia is tall and thin. Her face is brown and wrinkled; she wears large tortoise-shell spectacles and is square-jawed.

She was wearing a straw hat, an apron, and slippers on her bare feet.

She said, 'What did the doctor say, about your mother?'

'High blood pressure,' I said.

'Eh?'

'High blood pressure.'

'High, high,' said my mother, appearing. 'Very high.'

'Then no more meat,' said Signora Bottiglia.

My mother asked her to come in and have some coffee.

'Yesterday,' said my mother, 'I could feel a sort of hard lump in my throat which rasped me. This morning I seem to be all right.'

The two of them sat down in the kitchen, and my

mother poured out from a coffee-pot robed in a knitted cosy.

'But with high blood pressure,' said Signora Bottiglia, 'you should not take coffee. No more meat, no more coffee.'

My mother likes coffee.

'What am I to have, then, in the morning? When I get up in the morning, my stomach is as cold as ice. Anyhow, how can you do without stockings?'

Signora Bottiglia had raised one foot and was looking at her bronzed leg; along her calf was a swollen vein, of a bluish colour.

'And you have got a varicose vein,' said my mother. 'You are mad to go about like this in the morning, with this cold weather.'

'It isn't a varicose vein,' said Signora Bottiglia, squeezing the vein with her finger. 'It does not trouble me at all.'

'And what is it if it is not a varicose?' said my mother.

'Where is Giuliana?' I said.

'Giuliana,' said Signora Bottiglia, 'was up early. Gigi Sartorio came to fetch her, and they have gone to the tennis club.'

'What, to the tennis club?' said my mother, 'when Gigi has got his arm in plaster?'

'They are not playing, just looking on. Some matches are being played.'

'Ah, they are looking on,' said my mother. 'And why don't you go too, Elsa, to look on for a little?'

'I have to catch the bus at midday,' I said.

'Ah, of course, it is Saturday,' said my mother. 'Previously she used to go down to the town only on Wednesdays,' she explained to Signora Bottiglia, 'but now Saturdays as well. To change the book for Ottavia, who reads a lot.'

'Buy me a small packet of brewers' yeast,' said Signora Bottiglia. 'I want to make a *torta paradiso* tomorrow. We are having Purillo to dinner.'

'Purillo all by himself?' My mother was astonished.

'Yes, because Raffaella has gone to the sea with Pepè. He has had a horrid bad throat, that Pepè. Two tonsils like raspberries.'

'Pepè has always got one,' said my mother, feeling her neck. 'It is curious that if I squeeze hard it still hurts me. It will be my tonsils, maybe.'

'And after she has done her commissions,' said my mother, 'Elsa always goes and spends the afternoon with her friends, the Campanas.'

I have known the Campanas since university days.

'They have a beautiful house in the Via Novara,' said my mother. 'They are very well off.'

'The Campanas?' said Signora Bottiglia.

'The Campanas.'

'The children know them, too, the Campanas,' said

Signora Bottiglia. 'But he has had a coronary, and is in a clinic at present.'

'A coronary, has he?' said my mother. 'And how is it you have said nothing about it to me?' she said to me. 'When did he get this coronary?'

'Last month,' said Signora Bottiglia.

'A coronary? Consalvo Campana?'

'Consalvo Campana.'

'But you, how is it you have told me nothing about this coronary?' she said to me, when Signora Bottiglia had gone back to her hoeing in her sun hat.

'It was a small one,' I said.

'Small! A small coronary? . . .

'Small or big, they have taken him to a clinic,' she began again after a little while. 'And how is it you have told me nothing? I should have written a note, sent some flowers. The Campanas are always so nice to you.'

'I sent flowers,' I said.

'Ah, you sent some. What flowers?'

'Roses.'

'What colour?'

'White.'

'But one sends white roses to brides or when they have a baby,' said my mother. 'Carnations would be better, for a man.

'And where did you find roses at this time of

year?' she said. 'You must have spent a fortune, you must.'

While I was getting ready in my room Giuliana Bottiglia came in.

'Am I disturbing you?' she said.

She was wearing a white pleated skirt and a white pullover, and had a scarf over her shoulders on which was printed the map of London.

'London?' I said.

'London, yes. Gigi Sartorio brought it for me the last time he was there.'

'What does Gigi Sartorio go to London for?'

'Business.'

'What sort of business?'

'Business. I don't know.'

'Is Gigi Sartorio serious?'

'No. Merely a friend.'

'Were the matches good?'

'Good, yes. They beat the team from Cignano. Terenzi lost.'

'He always loses.'

'Not always. He lost today.'

She was sitting down and was arranging her hair with her comb.

'I am not your friend any more, isn't that true?' she said.

'Oh, do stop that.'

'We used to be friends once. You had no secrets from me.'

She said, 'Is he your boy, really?'

I was bending down and looking under the bed for my shoes.

'I must go or the bus will start,' I said.

'He is your boy, I know it.'

We were now walking down by the path. In my string bag I was carrying the books of the 'Selecta' library, bound in blue.

'If at least you looked happy,' she said, 'I would not ask you anything. But you don't seem a bit happy.'

She said, 'Sometimes I watch you go by at the garden gate, and you have a way of walking by which one can tell you are not happy.

'You push your hair back, take long strides, and look defiant. But all the time you have a sad expression.'

'Is it true that Gigi Sartorio takes morphine?' I asked.

'He doesn't take any morphine. He is taking an anodyne at the present time, because his arm hurts him.'

'I have been waiting for you for more than an hour,' said Tommasino.

'I missed the midday bus, and had to wait for the next one.'

'And how did you miss the bus?'

'I was with Giuliana Bottiglia, and she would stay with me and talk, and so I was late.'

'Why do you waste time with that stupid woman?'

'She knows about you and me,' I said.

'She knows? How does she know?'

'Because they saw us in a bar, her sister Maria and Maria Mosso.'

'And what do they say about us, all these Marias?'

'I don't know,' I said. 'Giuliana thinks that I don't look happy.'

'She is a stupid woman.'

'Why? Anyhow, do I seem happy?'

'I don't know what you seem,' he said.

'Don't you think that is horrid, not to know.'

'It doesn't seem to be horrid or not. I don't trouble myself with the problem.'

'Thanks,' I said.

'Thanks for what?'

'Thanks, just like that. . . .

'How hateful you can be,' I said. 'What a hateful person you can be.'

We were in the Via Gorizia and I said,

'I don't care about going upstairs today.'

'What have we come along here for then?'

I walked and he followed. I walked without any purpose, swinging the string bag with the books.

'Give me the bag,' he said. 'I will carry it. At least we can leave it with the porter in the Via Gorizia, damned string bag. Isn't your granny fed up with reading all those novels?'

'She's not my granny,' I said. 'She is my aunt.'

'Aunt or granny,' he said, 'what of it?'

'You know perfectly well that she is my aunt,' I said. 'You are as exact as a registrar's clerk and have a diabolical memory. You just said that to annoy me.'

'Of course,' he said and smiled, 'I know she is not your granny, she is your aunt. I said it out of temper, because I have been waiting for you, and I don't like waiting. . . .

'I got sick of that beastly doorway of the 'Selecta' library while I was waiting for you,' he said.

'I was afraid,' he said, 'something had happened to you. That you were ill, or perhaps the bus had crashed.'

He said, 'So the little Bottiglia girl thinks you don't look happy? . . .

'But why aren't you happy?' he said.

'When I am at home at Casa Tonda,' he said, 'I look towards your house. I look and wonder, "What will she be doing now? Is she sad or happy?". . .

'Does it please you that I think in that way when I am there alone? . . .

'You think it is little,' he said, 'that I give you. Little in the way of love?'

'Yes,' I said, 'it seems to me little in the way of love.'

'Yet it is all I can give you,' he said. 'I cannot give you more. I am not a romantic. I have a solitary nature. I stand alone. I have no friends, I do not look for any.

'Women,' he said, 'are happy with passionate romantic men.

'I was in despair a little while ago, waiting for you at the street corner. I said, "What shall I do if she does not come? Supposing she is dead?"

' "If she is dead," I said, "how shall I live?" '

We were now in the park and walked among the bare trees, treading the grass scorched by the frost.

'That room in the Via Gorizia,' he said, 'is ghastly. We could get another room in a nicer street. We could take a whole house. Can anyone stop us?

'Would you like us,' he said, 'to look for a house, a nice convenient one, with a kitchen, where we can cook up something to eat?'

'But is it worth while for so short a time?' I said. 'Only two afternoons, Wednesdays and Saturdays?'

'Why shouldn't it be worth while? Isn't it worth while to be comfortable, even for a few hours?

'Would you like us to go to Via Gorizia now, just for a little?' he said.

I had just got home, and was having my supper at the kitchen table. My mother was emptying the string bag on the table, taking out the books from the 'Selecta' one by one. She looked at a title-page with a scornful expression.

'Cat on a Hot Tin Roof,' she said. 'Oh, poor creature.

'And where's the brewers' yeast?' she said. 'Have you forgotten it?'

'Yes.'

'What was the brewers' yeast for?' said Aunt Ottavia. 'We haven't got to make a tart.'

'But it was not for us, it was for the Villa Bottiglia,' said my mother. 'The little girls there always remember when one gives them commissions.'

There was a ring at the garden gate.

'And who can that be, at this hour?' said my mother. 'It is almost eleven. Oh dear, it will be a telegram.'

Antonia took the great rusty key off its nail, and went to open the garden gate.

'Be quick, be quick,' said my mother, 'it will be a telegram.'

'It is the gentleman from the Casa Tonda,' said

Antonia, hanging the key on the nail again. 'I have shown him into the sitting-room.'

'From the Casa Tonda? What gentleman?' said my mother.

I went into the sitting-room and my mother followed me. Tommasino was standing there in his short overcoat, which was unbuttoned, with a small packet in his hand.

'The brewers' yeast,' he said. 'I kept it in my pocket.'

'Ah, the yeast,' said my mother. 'You should not have put yourself out for a small thing like that, Tommasino, at this hour.'

'Sit down,' she said.

My father appeared at the door with his pipe.

'Oh, good evening, my dear Tommasino,' he said.

My father was fond of Tommasino because he had been fond of Balotta, with whom he had been in the first war, on the Carso.

'Can we offer you something, Tommasino?' said my mother.

She said, 'So you met today in the town and did the shopping together?'

She was sitting in an arm-chair and arranging the embroidered collar on her breast.

'And how is your aunt, Magna Maria? I must go to see her, one of these days. She has promised to teach me *petit point.* She makes rugs and bedspreads of *petit point.* She is so industrious, so splendid, how splendid she is,' she said, entering into the vein of Magna Maria.

'Have you had any supper, Tommasino?' I said.

'I? Yes, and you, dear?'

'Ah, you are on intimate terms. Of course, you have known each other since you were little children,' said my mother.

'You used to play together,' she said, 'as children in Magna Maria's garden. And Barba Tommaso used to take you to climb on those rocks, behind the house, just where they killed Nebbia, poor fellow,'

'I don't remember,' I said.

'I remember a little,' said Tommasino. 'You had some long pinafores, all with bows.'

'They were horrible, those pinafores,' I said.

'They were very pretty,' said my mother. 'I embroidered them myself. I like embroidery. But I have never learnt *petit point.*'

'We played together two or three times, at the most,' I said.

'And then you lost sight of one another,' said my mother. 'It seems strange, one lives two steps away—it is a nutshell of a village—and yet we never see each other. We don't see much of anyone any more. Just occasionally the Bottiglias. The brewers' yeast was for them. I don't use it. I find I get on better with Angel's Foam.'

'What is Angel's Foam? What a romantic name,' said my father.

'Angel's Foam,' said Aunt Ottavia, 'is nothing but brewers' yeast.'

She had come into the room and sat down in a corner, and had the books, bound in blue, on her knees.

'Brewers' yeast, Angel's Foam? But you are crazy!' said my mother.

'Were the books we got all right?' said Tommasino.

'Ah, then you went together to the "Selecta" as well,' said my mother. 'It is a good library, the "Selecta," everything is there, including foreign novels. My sister reads a great deal; I cannot, I haven't the time; I am too much taken up with the house, and am never still a minute. Then I have too much to think about, too many worries. I never stay still a minute, and cannot lose myself in a novel. My children are so far away. Do you remember my Giampiero, Tommasino?'

'I remember him,' said Tommasino. 'How is he?'

There he was sitting, with his hands over his knees with a polite subdued air, quite at home.

'He has got a splendid position,' said my mother,

'at Caracas in Venezuela. He would have liked to work in the factory here, but he and Guascogna the engineer did not get on together, and so he has gone all that distance away.'

Guascogna the engineer is Purillo.

'If your father was still here and poor Vincenzino, it would be different,' said my mother. 'Poor Vincenzino, what a sad end!'

She said, 'There are so many sad things in life. Why read novels? Is not life a novel?'

She said, 'You know that my Teresita has ended up in South Africa? You remember her? She is a mother now. Even down there such a lot happens, I am never at ease; I have worries and things to think about; my head always hurts me, just here on the back of the neck in the brain. I went yesterday to the doctor's, with Elsa, he thought me quite worn out, and found I had high blood pressure. This new doctor is splendid; he is very careful, and exact, and writes everything down. Today, however, I have felt well all the time, only I have a rasping feeling in the throat, as though I had swallowed some nails—it must be my tonsils.'

'I have got some penicillin lozenges at home,' said Tommasino, 'for throat troubles. I will bring some tomorrow for you if you believe in it.'

'Ah, penicillin?' said my mother. 'I am rather allergic to penicillin, to tell you the truth. Perhaps because I know that it is made of mould. They cure people now with mould—that is strange.'

She said, 'Why don't you come to supper tomorrow? Bring those lozenges for me. I will try them; perhaps they will do me good.'

She said, 'And Guascogna the engineer, how is he? And Raffaella? And Pepè? He has had a sore throat, too, hasn't he? I mean Pepè? And so they have taken him to the sea? I wonder if the sea would do me good, too? But how can I leave the house, to go to the sea? And then we have not got so much money to spend. For high blood pressure now, will the sea be any good?"

I took the key from its nail and went with Tommasino to the garden gate.

'Did I behave properly?' he asked.

'Properly, oh yes. You were ridiculous.'

'I was ridiculous? Weren't you pleased?'

'Why did you come?' I asked.

He said, 'To bring the brewers' yeast.

'I came,' he said, 'to try it out.'

'To try it out?'

'Yes, to try it out.'

'To try out seeing me in my picture frame?'

'Yes.'

'And what impression did I make on you, in my picture frame?'

'I, too. What impression did I make on you in your picture frame?'

My mother on the steps was asking whether or not we should invite Gigi Sartorio to supper along with Tommasino.

'Perhaps no,' she said, 'because of that arm. What impression would a guest make at table with an arm stretched out on a board?

'But how is it that you told me you had forgotten it, the yeast? You had not forgotten it; you had bought it and given it to Tommasino.'

'What a handsome young man,' said Aunt Ottavia.

'Handsome, yes. Of all Balotta's children he has always been the best-looking,' said my mother.

She said, 'But what put it into your head to take him back to the "Selecta"?'

She said, 'But what put it into his head to come here so late, just for a bit of yeast? The result is I had to invite him to supper. I shall make him a spinach soufflé. And a *zabaione*. I can make a *zabaione* as well if I do not invite Gigi Sartorio, because they had it yesterday evening.'

'Too many eggs,' said Aunt Ottavia; 'eggs in the soufflé, eggs in the *zabaione*. Better to finish with a fruit tart.'

'A fruit tart? And aren't there eggs in that?'

'Tommasino,' said my mother, 'have a little more soufflé. It is very light.'

She said, 'I wanted to ask Gigi Sartorio as well. But I did not know if you would have liked that. And then he is handicapped at the moment with that arm. One fears all the time that he might knock up against something.'

She said, 'Gigi Sartorio is rather odd. They say he is a morphine addict. I wonder if it is true.

'Do you, Tommasino, believe it?

'They say he has some odd tastes,' said my mother again. 'He goes abroad a lot, and will have picked up queer habits, perhaps. I wonder. His father, the General, is a very distinguished person.

'They say he has strange tastes. I don't know. You know him well, Tommasino?'

'General Sartorio?'

'No, no, the son. The General surely has not got strange tastes. He is such a methodical man.'

'They say in the village,' said Aunt Ottavia, 'that Gigi Sartorio is engaged to Giuliana Bottiglia.'

'Just imagine it!' said my mother. 'They are merely good friends, good companions. For example, the other morning he came to fetch her and they went to the tennis club to watch. Do you play tennis, Tommasino?'

'No,' said Tommasino, 'I don't go in for any sport.'

'That's bad,' said my mother, 'because you are tall, and have an athlete's figure. Our Elsa here formerly used to go to the tennis club. She played well; they said she had a long reach, a fine reach. But she has given up going. I wonder why.

'And my Giampiero,' she said, 'when he was here was passionately fond of sport. Nowadays in Venezuela he has grown lazy; it must be the climate. Indeed, when he came on leave I saw that he had lost his good colour.

'You, too, Tommasino,' she said, 'haven't at all a good colour. You are always a bit pale. Perhaps it is the sedentary life you lead.'

'I am all right for colour,' said Tommasino.

'No, you are not all right. As a child you were white and red, an apple.'

'One of the little Bottiglia girls is engaged then?' said Tommasino.

'Ah, you call them the little Bottiglia girls, too?' said my mother. 'I thought that it was only we who called them that, at home here. They are not little girls any more, by any means.'

'Why "by any means"?' said my father.

'By any means,' said my mother, 'because they are not yet married. For a woman marriage is the finest destiny, a happy marriage. Not an unfortunate one, otherwise it is better with nothing, one knows that.

You, Tommasino, have had the sad experience of an unfortunate marriage in your family. Poor Vincenzino.

'And perhaps it is for that reason,' she said, 'that you don't get married. You will think long about it and you are right. For that matter, as a man, you are still very young.'

'I,' said Aunt Ottavia, 'have not married, and I am quite happy so.'

'You were not cut out for marriage,' said my mother; 'you are too fond of your own convenience.'

'My convenience? And when do I ever look after my own convenience?' said Aunt Ottavia.

'Well, she has not got engaged, Giuliana Bottiglia,' said my mother; 'one has seen them about together for years, she and Gigi Sartorio. If they were engaged, I should be the first to know of it. Her mother, Netta Bottiglia, and I are together from morning till evening.'

'How is your work getting on, my dear Tommasino?' asked my father.

Twisting his hair round his fingers, Tommasino began to talk about linear programmation.

We went into the sitting-room for coffee.

'Your views are socialistic, aren't they, Tommasino?' said my mother. 'Is this linear programmation, if I have understood it rightly, something socialistic?'

I could not allow my mother to appropriate linear programmation.

'Socialism does not come into it at all,' I said. 'It is useless to wish to talk about what one doesn't understand.'

'I have understood it perfectly well,' said my mother. 'My poor brother—I don't know if you have heard him mentioned, Tommasino—was also taken up with these matters. He died some years ago; his name was Cesare Maderna.'

'Your brother,' said my father, 'was employed on the railways. How could he have had anything to do with what Tommasino was talking about?'

'But he was a politician,' said my mother. 'He was a candidate for Parliament. He was a Socialist. A great Socialist like your father, Tommasino.'

'Except, however, that he joined the Fascist Party,' said my father.

'What does that matter? He had to do it or he lost his place. From every point of view he was first a politician and was interested in social problems, exactly as Tommasino is now. Isn't that true, Ottavia?

'Our poor brother,' said Aunt Ottavia, 'was only a humble railway employee. As a young man he took some part in politics, without much success, however. He was never a candidate for Parliament. You, Matilda, confuse him with Cousin Ernesto. Cousin

Ernesto, yes, was a candidate for Parliament. But our poor brother, never. He was just an honourable man. He did join the Fascists, yes, but as for the black shirt he never put it on. He had one, but he never put it on.'

'And what did it matter to him even if he did lose his place?' said my father. 'His wife was rich; he would go on just the same. His wife,' said he, turning to Tommasino, 'was a Terenzi of Cignano. Vineyards, woods, pastures, a fine inheritance. They had no children and left everything on their death to the priests.'

'That was she, his wife,' said my mother. 'He could not bear to look at the priests. But he was already dead when she died.'

'A Terenzi of Cignano,' said Tommasino. 'Relations of the Terenzis of this place?'

'Distant relations.'

'And on the other hand, as regards Cousin Ernesto,' said Aunt Ottavia, the Fascists beat him up, and he was in prison, too. He died poor.'

'And our cousin's daughter,' said my mother, 'had a very beautiful voice. She went to America and sang in the biggest theatres. Then, suddenly, she lost her voice. Now she cannot sing any more, not even *Garibaldi's Hymn.*'

'That is because she was in a fire over there, in America,' said Aunt Ottavia. 'The hotel caught fire one night and she had to jump from the window, and everyone called out to her to jump, and she stuck there astride of the window-sill and would not jump. At last she jumped, because they had spread the safety net, you know, underneath. She jumped, but she lost her voice.'

'Partly fear, partly the smoke,' said my mother.

'Now, however,' said Aunt Ottavia, 'she has consoled herself and married a dentist.'

'Because after she had lost her voice,' said my mother, 'she went practically mad through grief and was treated in a clinic. Once a week a dentist visited the place to see the patients' teeth, and thus he fell in love with her. She had a very beautiful mouth.'

'So, we have heard the whole story of Cousin Ernesto's daughter,' said my father.

'Ada, don't you remember Ada?' said my mother. 'We have not seen her again for years and years. But she was a tall, beautiful woman.'

'You have told this story to me millions of times,' said my father. 'Why do you want to bother Tommasino with it, with persons he has never seen and never will see?'

'It serves to make a bit of conversation,' said my mother. 'Do you want us to sit here all evening gazing into each other's eyes? One tells stories and talks, someone says one thing, and someone else another.'

She said, 'Tommasino, do you want me to sew that button on your sleeve? You will lose it otherwise.'

She said, 'This overcoat is almost done for. Why don't you tell Gigi Sartorio to bring you a montgomery from London the next time he goes there? They are very practical.'

She said, 'You are not offended with me for saying this? I am a regular mother, am I not?'

'He has been very well brought up,' said my mother to my father when they were alone in their room. I heard them through the wall.

'You see,' said my mother, 'that Salice school is a good school.

'Perhaps he is not as odd as all that,' she said. 'Perhaps the little oddities he has are faults of youth.'

'He is very likeable,' she said. 'He has Signora Cecilia's nose. His mouth is that of Magna Maria.'

'I don't see any trace of Magna Maria in Tommasino,' said my father.

'Because you don't understand resemblances,' said my mother.

'Well, then, what impression did I make on you in my own picture frame?' I said.

We were in the room in the Via Gorizia, and I was

lying on the bed. Tommasino was sitting up to the table with his elbows on it, and smoking.

'An unfavourable impression, yes?' I said.

'And I,' he said, 'what impression did I make in your picture frame?' he said.

'You are always in my frame,' I said. 'You never leave it.

'I keep you there always,' I said, 'among my things, and I talk to you and everything goes on just as when we are together here. But you, you put me away from yourself. You go back to your Casa Tonda, and I am not there. Occasionally, but only occasionally, you look down towards my house. But only occasionally and, as it were, by mistake.

'I do not,' I said, 'put you away from me. I keep you there among my things. If I did not, there are times when I could not put up with my picture frame.'

'You put up with it,' he said, 'before I existed for you.'

'Yes, I did,' I said. 'It irked me, but I put up with it. But I did not know then that life could have another pace. I imagined one vaguely, but I did not know.

'I did not know,' I said, 'that life could go at a run, with drums beating.

'For you, it is different,' I said. 'Your life, after I came into it, went on at its usual pace, without any sound.'

'There is a little sound,' he said, 'a little, yes, for me. Not really loud, but it is there.'

He said, 'But I should have liked to have gone far away, somewhere abroad, and to have got to know you by chance, in some street or other, a girl one had never seen before. I should like to know nothing about you, nothing of your relations and not to meet them ever.'

'Instead,' I said, 'we have grown up in the same village, and played together as children, at Le Pietre. But that does not worry me at all. To me it is of no significance.'

I said, 'It is of no significance to me. And since you have come to exist for me, our village there has become an unknown land, very big and all full of unforeseeable dramatic things that stir the emotions and can happen at any moment. It can happen to me, for example, to cross the piazza to the post and to see your car standing outside the Concordia, or to see your sisters or to see Magna Maria.'

'I don't understand,' he said. 'Do you find your emotions stirred at seeing Magna Maria?'

'Seeing Magna Maria,' I said, 'makes my heart beat quickly.'

'I don't understand. When I meet your father in the corridor at the works I don't feel my heart beating.

'I have a great regard for your father,' he said, 'but I swear to you that he does not make my heart beat fast!'

'Because you are not in love with me,' I said. 'That is the sole explanation.

'There is no change in your life,' I said, 'since the day when I came to exist for you.

'It is for this reason,' I said, 'that you go on day-dreaming about supposing you had met me in a foreign country, supposing everything had happened differently. For me, on the other hand, it is all right just as it happened. We played together as children with those ugly pinafores.'

'It was you that had ugly pinafores,' he said. 'I have never worn pinafores in my life.'

'I said you were not romantic,' I said, 'and it is not true—you are romantic. You want veiled ladies and unknown cities, not families or parents. This means being a romantic.'

'I have got so many, so many relations,' he said, 'a long trail of them.

'I have a trail of relations like a long snake,' he said. 'I should not want any more, no. My own are enough.'

'When you came to my home, the other evening, with the yeast, you said you wanted to try it out. What did you want to try out?

'You wanted to try out,' I said, 'being my fiancé and you saw that it did not suit you? You don't like it?'

'I saw,' he said, 'that it was a bit difficult for me.'

'And so now it will no longer be nice to come here either,' I said, 'now that we have been together there in my home, with my parents, first in the sitting-room, then in the dining-room, then in the sitting-room again. Now that you have had coffee in our pretty flowered cups, now that you have heard the stories about Cousin Ernesto, it seems to me that I shall no longer enjoy being with you here, in this room, or changing the books at the "Selecta" or going for walks with you in the park, because I shall always be thinking of how you wanted to try out being my fiancé, and it didn't suit you and you didn't like it. I shall always think that I am all right for you here as a girl friend, but I am not all right for you as a wife.'

'I have always told you,' he said, 'that I did not wish to marry you.'

'True,' I said. 'You have always said that. And I said, "Patience." I suffered for it, but I said, "Patience. It's better than nothing,"' I said. 'But now you have tried it out; you wanted to see if by chance you were not making a mistake. And you saw that you were making a mistake, and that you could not go on. And now in the face of that I can no longer say, "Patience." It hurts me in a way which I do not know how to bear.'

I said, 'I felt so happy that you had come to my home, that evening, with the yeast, and I was so glad to see you there large as life in our little sitting-room where I was always thinking of you. But instead everything now is ruined. Now we cannot be here either. I have come to hate this Via Gorizia, this room.'

And I began to cry. I said,

'Why have we ruined everything?'

'Ah, no,' he said, 'don't cry. I hate to see women cry.'

But I cried and said just like Catè,

'Why has everything been ruined?'

The next day in the evening Tommasino came to speak to my father. He had put on dark clothes. He had consulted Betta and Betta had told him that dark clothes were indispensable.

My father opened a bottle of moscado for the occasion, from our own vineyard, nine years old.

My mother was so moved that she remained awake all night. She woke my father and said to him,

'Had you thought of him?'

And she said,

'When he appeared before me the other evening with that packet in his hand, I thought of it.'

Then she said,

'But the property, what will that amount to? It must be a fine figure, eh?'

My father, half asleep, said,

'I don't know.'

'You don't know? You, the accountant, don't know? A fine accountant! Well, then, who is there who does know?'

First thing in the morning she ran to tell the whole story to Signora Bottiglia. But Signora Bottiglia knew all about it, because Betta had told her when she came in the early morning with the vegetables.

Indeed, she knew even earlier than that that there was something. She had known of it for some time.

Her daughter Mariolina had told her that she had seen me and Tommasino one day in the city, sitting in a café, holding hands.

'Impossible,' said my mother, 'just imagine to yourself whether Elsa would let her hands be held by a man in public. I wonder what your Maria can have seen.'

She was a bit puzzled, because Signora Bottiglia had not shown surprise, and she had a zest for creating surprises and the whole night she had been anticipating the pleasure of seeing surprise in her old friend's eyes, behind their big lenses, always lit up with a little green sparkle either of incredulity or malice.

Signora Bottiglia said,

'We mothers are always the last to know these things.'

And she told as a secret to my mother that her daughter Giuliana was about to get engaged to Gigi Sartorio. But they were waiting because they must first take off the plaster of Paris.

'How does the plaster come into it?' asked my mother. 'There is not the slightest need of his arm to get engaged with.'

'But the doctor,' said Signora Bottiglia, 'has advised that he should not get excited, or perspire, or jerk himself.'

'There are no jerks in getting engaged,' said my mother. 'There is no need at all to perspire.'

On getting home she hastened to tell Aunt Ottavia about Giuliana and Gigi.

'It will rather be that he has to wait to be quite cured of his morphine before he marries, that's what it will be.'

7

The End of the Affair

TOMMASINO took to coming to us every evening. In the winter there were heavy falls of snow, and he would arrive with his hair full of snow, and my mother would say,

'Why do you go about without a hat?'

Sometimes he played a card game with my father. Sometimes we sat in the sitting-room, he and I and Aunt Ottavia, who read her novels.

My mother would say,

'I am leaving your aunt here; it is usual for someone to be with an engaged couple.'

She referred to my aunt as though she was a chair. And as a matter of fact Aunt Ottavia behaved like a chair, silent, motionless. She did not raise her eyes from her book.

Still, she was there, and we could find nothing to say to each other because of the presence of that head and its woolly tresses there under the lamp.

He twisted his hair round his fingers. I knitted.

It just seemed to me impossible that a Via Gorizia

could have ever existed, and a room with a little stove behind a curtain where we sometimes made coffee.

We still went often to the town. But we did not go any more to the Via Gorizia. On the contrary, we avoided going down that street.

I did not know either if he still kept that room on or continued to pay the rent.

We avoided certain topics. We rarely spoke of the old times when we met there in the Via Gorizia. Both of us pretended that those times had never existed.

We used to go to the furniture and upholstery shops to satisfy my mother.

And my mother would ask,

'Have you ordered the sideboard and shelves? Have you been to see that divan?'

Then my mother took it into her head to come with us every time that we went down into the town. She walked about very slowly, stopping at every shop window, and the hours became interminable.

My mother wanted pictures and carpets for the Casa Tonda. She wanted to pack it from top to bottom so that there should not be a square inch left uncovered.

At night when she could not get to sleep she let her imagination run ahead. She played the devil with the Casa Tonda, broke down walls, had floors up, erected colonnades and arcades, converted loggias into baths and baths into loggias. Also, between sleeping and waking, she dismissed Betta. Betta had told Signora Bottiglia that Tommasino deserved a prettier and richer wife than myself, and Signora Bottiglia had immediately reported this to my mother. So my mother dismissed Betta, imagining to herself a scene in which she caught her stealing. She spoke a few sharp contemptuous words to Betta, and appointed in her place the old nurse, Gemmina's old nurse, promising her a big increase of wages. She did this to spite Gemmina as well, since she did not like her.

Gemmina had asked us to dinner, me and Tommasino, and had given us rabbit. My mother considered that a great lack of respect. Rabbit seemed to her by no means a choice dish, not by any means intended to celebrate an engagement.

And on one occasion when my mother had been to call on her at the Casetta, tiring her legs out on the way up, Gemmina had unloaded on her four tickets for the arts and crafts exhibition and a very ugly little tablecloth with tassels which cost eight hundred lire.

Next, my mother, between sleeping and waking, dismissed Purillo from the works, I don't know how, and put Tommasino in his place. She changed the whole organization of the works and increased the workers' pay. On the other hand, she reduced Borzaghi's salary, because she did not like Borzaghi, having quarrelled with his wife on some occasion, in a shop, when Signora Borzaghi had wished to be served first.

My mother had somewhat forgotten her ailments in the excitement, and when she remembered them she blamed Gemmina for a cold which she felt in her bronchial tubes, after that day when she went to La Casetta and had got hot on the way up and there had been a breeze.

We were invited, I and Tommasino, once or twice to supper at Le Pietre. Barba Tommaso pointed at me with his finger and shouted,

'But who is she? Who is she?'

And Magna Maria kissed me loudly on the cheeks and said,

'Splendid, splendid!'

On the way back Tommasino asked,

'Do you still find it moving to see Magna Maria?'

And I said,

'Much less.'

'Then,' said he, 'you have become more like me because I have never felt moved at seeing members of your family.'

And he asked me,

'Anyway are you happy?'

And I said,

'Yes.'

The days were running on with ever-increasing rapidity of rhythm, impetuous and deep, and the whole of my life was going forward with drums beating. The drums beat so loud within me as to be deafening.

Tommasino and I used to go for walks in the country. The snow was beginning to melt, but there were still traces here and there to which the sun gave a rosy tinge.

He said, 'It is nicer here than in the park. We have had so many walks in the park and through the town. In contrast it is nicer here. Yes? No?'

He said, 'Yet you are not happy. It is true that you are not so happy?'

And I said, 'Yes, it is true.'

But I could not explain why.

He said, 'Then what do you want?'

He said, 'You wanted me to marry you and I am marrying you. What else do you want?'

I said, 'I don't know.'

He said, 'How complicated you are! How complicated and tiresome women are!'

He said, 'And at the house one of those little evenings awaits us in the sitting-room with Aunt Ottavia?'

He said, 'And tomorrow we have to go into town with your mother to look at divans?'

He said, 'But if only you were happy at least!

Instead, no, you are not happy, and I don't know what you want.'

We were to be married in July.

We had gone down one afternoon to town, the two of us alone, without my mother, who had stayed at home to do some work on a big Spanish shawl of black lace, out of which she wanted to make a dress for the wedding.

It was also Corpus Christi day; all the shops were closed and we had nothing in particular to do. Only, Tommasino had to look in for a moment at the tailor's for a second fitting of the new suit which he had ordered, a tailor whose name Purillo had given him.

So we went in there and I sat in a little room to wait for him. Then Tommasino appeared to let me see the suit. The jacket was all full of basting stitches and the collar was a piece of canvas.

He walked up and down in front of the looking glass, and the tailor followed him with his mouth full of pins. It was a dark suit which he was to wear at the reception in our house, the evening before the wedding.

After that we walked about the town and ended up at the park. Tommasino was mimicking the tailor who spoke with *e* in the place of *a*, being from Bari.

He said, 'Purillo must have a boy friend from Bari,

because he is always giving me addresses of people from there; a garage owner to whom he sent me was also a man from Bari.'

He said, 'I wonder how Purillo finds them out, all these men from Bari?'

We had been the previous evening to supper at the Villa Rondine.

I said, 'Do you think Raffaella is happy with Purillo?'

He said, 'No, I think she is profoundly unhappy. She only has Pepè.'

He said, 'How could you want her to be happy with Purillo?'

I said, 'Why didn't you try to talk to her, to make her talk? To help her a little?'

'Because I should not achieve anything,' he said. 'On the contrary, if I talked to her and made her talk, I should make her still more unhappy. Do you think it is possible to help another person?

'Nothing can be done, not for others,' he said.

'Raffaella certainly does not think about being unhappy,' he said; 'she has driven all her thoughts underground. She is unhappy, but takes care not to admit it to herself, so as to be able to live.

'Besides,' he said, 'it always ends with living like that.'

'You, too,' I asked, 'with time going on, will you

end with driving your thoughts underground? Do you believe that yourself?'

'Of course,' he said. 'In fact, in some ways I have already begun. Otherwise, how would you manage?

'In these months,' he said, 'I have driven a great many of my thoughts underground. I have dug out a little grave for them.'

'What do you mean?' I said. 'In these months, in these last months, since you have been engaged to me?'

'Why, yes, of course,' he said. 'You know that yourself, too. We are practically always silent, now, together. We remain almost always silent, because we have begun to drive our thoughts underground, right at the bottom, right at the bottom inside ourselves. Then when we begin talking again, we only say things of no account.

'Formerly,' he said, 'I told you everything that came into my head. Not any more, now. Now I have lost the wish to tell you things. What I think about now, I tell a little of it to myself, and then I bury it. I send it underground. Then, little by little, I shall not tell things any more even to myself. I shall drive everything underground at once, every random thought, before it can take shape.'

'But that,' I said, 'means being unhappy.'

'Undoubtedly,' he said, 'it means being very unhappy. But it happens to so many people. A person at a certain moment will not look his own soul in the face any more. Because he is afraid, if he looks it in the face, of not having the courage to go on living any more.'

'And you have been all these months,' I said, 'realizing that this was happening to you, and watching how it happened. This is what you were thinking about while we were in the sitting-room in the evening, with Aunt Ottavia? You were turning your back on your own soul?'

'Of course,' he said, 'that was what I was thinking about there in the sitting-room. What else but that?'

We were walking in the park by the river. There was a crowd, noise and music, and they had set up a Luna Park on the lawns behind the castle.

People kept passing by us, or gathered together by the stone parapet which faces the river, and threw themselves on the grassy bank with cries and whistles, for the regatta was on that day.

Many boats were going up and down the river, with little flags fluttering in the wind. The shelter, too, on the landing stage, built on piles, was full of people, and little flags fluttered in the wind on its roof.

'Formerly,' he said, 'when we were up there in that room in the Via Gorizia, I always had the wish to tell you everything I was thinking about. It was fine; there was a great freedom, a sense of breathing fully.

Now that wish is entirely exhausted, in these months.'

'And do you think,' I said, 'that it will never come back?'

'Oh no,' he said, 'it is exhausted. How can it come back?

'Formerly,' he said, 'I could choose whether to be with you of an afternoon, or not. Now, on the other hand, in these months, I have felt that I could not choose any more, that I had to come to you without any escape, there to your home, because I had jolly well made my choice, once and for all. I had to do what everyone was expecting me to do, what you along with the others expected of me. So, I have taken to driving my thoughts underground. I could not look my soul in the face any more. To avoid hearing my soul cry aloud, I turned my back on it and walked away from it.'

'This is horrible,' I said. 'You have just told me something horrible.'

'Didn't you know it was horrible?' he said. 'You knew it, too, yourself. You knew that you had driven underground this self-awareness. You, too, have done what they all expected you to do. You went with your mother to the upholsterers, and furniture shops and linen shops. And all the time inside yourself you could hear the long cries of your soul, but always farther off, always fainter, always covered with more earth.'

'Then,' said I, 'why did we become engaged? Why are we getting married?'

'To be like everyone,' he said, 'and to do what everyone expects of us.

'My love for you,' he said, 'was not a great love. You know that well. I have often told you it was not a great love, impassioned, romantic. There was something, all the same, something intimate and delicate, and it had its own fulfilment and its own freedom. You and I, up there in the Via Gorizia, alone, without any plans for the future, without anything at all, have been happy in some fashion of our own. We had something there; it was not much, but it was something. It was something very slight, very fragile, ready to break up at the first puff of wind. It was something which could not be captured and brought to the light or it would die. We have brought it to the light and it is dead, and we shall never recover it any more.

'Would you like to go up there in the Via Gorizia for a little while?' he asked. 'I have kept that room on all the time and paid the rent. I went there, you know, sometimes while you were with your mother at the dressmaker's or the draper's. I went there and had a little rest and sometimes made some coffee. I felt a great silence there, a great peace.

'Would you like to go there now for a little while?' he said.

'Oh no,' I said, 'it would be too depressing, Tommasino.

'Only one thing is clear,' I said. 'I am in love and you are not.

'I am in love,' I said, 'now, in the beginning and always, and you, no. You, never.'

We went to catch the bus. Not the last one. It was only five in the afternoon, the sun was not yet setting.

The bus was almost empty at that hour. We sat side by side, and talked no more.

The next morning I got up and dressed very quietly, without letting my mother hear me; and I went to the Casa Tonda.

I had never been there alone. I had been there, of course, with my mother, with Gemmina, or with Raffaella often.

Tommasino came to open the door for me. He was already up and dressed, although it was early; and he had put on a thick grey shaggy pullover, although outside a hot sunny day was beginning.

'*Salve*,' he said to me without showing any surprise. 'I am unwell, have caught a cold; I probably had a bit of a temperature last night. That is why I have put on this pullover.'

There he was in the dining-room, with his pullover

drawn down over his thin body, and the cuffs full of handkerchiefs.

He had a small sponge in his hand and was cleaning his tape-recorder.

'Do you want to speak something into the tape-recorder?' he said. 'Hearing one's own voice is interesting. To begin with I could not bear it; I found my voice horrid, falsetto. Then I got accustomed to it. But it is interesting. Try it.'

I said, 'No.'

I had sat down. I had my hands in my jacket pockets, and looked at him. I looked at him, I looked at his head, his ruffled hair, his long big pullover, his thin hands which could not keep still and made continuous gestures.

'I have come to return the ring to you,' I said.

I drew it out of my pocket; it was small with a small pearl; this ring which he had given to me had belonged to his mother, Signora Cecilia.

He took it and laid it on the table.

'You don't want to marry me,' he said.

'No,' I said. 'How can you think that I want to marry you still after the things that you said to me yesterday?'

'Yesterday,' he said, 'I was depressed, taking a gloomy view of things. I probably felt that I was going to have a temperature.

'However, of course,' he said, 'you are right; it is better so.'

I gazed round, and said,

'I have pictured everything, only too clearly. I have pictured you and me, here, in this room, in this house. I have pictured everything with great exactness down to the smallest details. And when one sees the things of the future so clearly as though they were already happening, it is a sign that they should never happen. They have already happened in a sense in our minds, and it is really not possible to experience them further.'

I said, 'It is like, on some days, the air is too clear, too transparent, and one sees everything sharply and exactly outlined, and then one will say that rain is coming.'

'How calm you are!' he said. 'You do not cry; you say everything so calmly.

'And I?' he said. 'What shall I do?'

'You will do as you have always done,' I said.

'And you?' he said. 'What will you do?'

'I, too, shall do as I have always done,' I said.

'How calm we are!' he said. 'How cool, quiet, calm!

'I hope,' he said twisting his hair round his fingers, 'that you may some day meet a better man than I am.'

'You see, it is not in me,' he said, 'no real vitality.

This is my great want. I feel a shudder of disgust when I should assert myself. I want to assert myself, and then I have this shudder. Anybody else, with a shudder like that—well, he does not take any account of it, he puts it out of his mind at once. But I keep it in my mind for a long time.

'It is because I have the feeling,' he said, 'that they have already lived enough, those others before me; that they have already consumed all the reserves, all the vitality that there was for us. The others, Nebbia, Vincenzino, my father. Nothing was left over for me.

'The others,' he said, 'all those who have lived in this village before me. It seems to me that I am only their shadow.'

He said, 'In earlier days, after Vincenzino died, I thought that I should have realized all his plans. He had heaps of them ready, designs for the factory, canteens, rest-rooms, quarters for the work-people. They were sensible, practicable things, not just dreams. He never had time to bring them to completion. I thought that I should do that myself.

'Instead,' he said, 'I have been no good at doing anything. I always say "yes" to Purillo. I have not the will to hold out against him, to contest. I knuckle under and say "yes".

'Sometimes,' he said, 'I have an idea of going away from this place. To find a bit of vitality.

'I shall go to Canada perhaps,' he said. 'Some time ago, last year, Borzaghi told me he could get me some work there, in Canada, at Montreal.'

'Canada,' said I. 'I don't know what it is like. I imagine that it must be a place full of wood.'

'Yes,' he said, and smiled, 'there must be quite a bit of wood there. Forests.'

One could see the Villa Rondine from the windows, one could see Purillo playing tennis in the garden with Borzaghi's son.

'Look at him there,' said Tommasino, gazing through the panes. 'Look at him there—Purillo, fine fellow. Now, he has got plenty of vitality, or rather he has not so much got it as that he behaves as if he had, and he gets the results he wants.

'Perhaps it is just because he is stupid,' he said, 'and he has never realized they have already exhausted all the vitality that was available in this place.

'How a place can get one down!' he said. 'It has a weight of lead, with all its dead. This village of ours, it just gets me down; it is so small, a handful of houses. I can never free myself from it, I cannot forget it. Even if I end up in Canada, I shall take it with me!

'If only you had been a girl,' he said, 'from another village! If only I had found you in Montreal or somewhere, if only we had met there and married! We should have felt so free, so unburdened, without these houses, these hills, these mountains. Free as a bird, I should have been!

'But even if I took you with me to Montreal now,' he said, 'it would be just like it is here; we should not be able to create anything new. We should probably still go on talking about Vincenzino and Nebbia and Purillo. It would be exactly the same as being here.

'After all, I wonder whether I shall ever go there, to Montreal,' he said.

'And now you must go along,' he said and he took my face between his hands. 'You must go, like this, without crying, without shedding even a single tear. Go along with dry eyes, quite open and calm. It is not worth while to shed tears, and I want to remember you like that.

'*Ciao*, good-bye, Elsa,' he said, and I said,

'*Ciao*, good-bye, Tommasino.'

And I came away.

In the days that followed Purillo came to see my father and explain to him that Tommasino and I had agreed for our own reasons to break off the engagement.

Breaking off engagements was jam for Purillo. He had formerly undertaken Vincenzino's affair with the Brazilian girl, Mamita's daughter, many years ago now.

He offered my father compensation for the expense to which he had been put. My father refused it coldly and was offended.

But he harboured no ill feeling for Tommasino. Besides, I told him that we were both agreed not to think of marrying any more, for our own reasons, and that there had not been any fault on either side. My father could not bear Tommasino any ill will, because he was fond of him, and continued even now to be fond of him. He was fond, too, of old Balotta and respected his memory.

My father told my mother to leave me in peace. He said that the young people of today had psychological problems of a subtle, complicated kind which it was not given to them, the old generation, to understand.

However, in those first days my father was very cast down. He felt an antipathy to the factory, and would not go there any more. He said that he was old now, and did not want to work any longer, and was going to retire and take it easy. He just took a post as consultant in a small way at Cignano with a firm of contractors.

When my mother knew about our breaking off she cried, fainted, and had to send for Signora Bottiglia, who stayed all night to look after her.

Then she set about having all the linen of my trousseau put away in the wardrobes. Coming one day on the Spanish shawl to which she had added velvet sleeves and which was now seen to be useless, she once more cried long and loud.

For some time, for some months, she refused to leave the house, feeling ashamed before other people.

In the village they said all sorts of things. They said that I had given up Tommasino because going early one morning to the Casa Tonda I had found him in bed with Betta's daughter, a child of only fifteen.

They said that I had given him up because my father in his capacity of accountant had discovered that the position of the factory was shaky.

They said that he had given me up because I had too many lovers.

They said that he had given me up because he had discovered that I took morphine, just like Gigi Sartorio.

I went for some months to Lambrate to stay with Cousin Ernesto's sister.

In the meantime Tommasino also had gone away; but he had not gone to Montreal. He had only gone as far as Liverpool for some months, to deal with certain business matters on Purillo's behalf.

When I came back from Lambrate they were no longer talking about me and Tommasino in the village.

They were talking about Giuliana Bottiglia and

Gigi Sartorio, who had meanwhile married, and had taken a large villa, a long way from his old father, whom they had left alone.

Now Tommasino has returned. In the evening I look across to the lights lit up in the Casa Tonda.

He has come back, and sometimes I meet him in the piazza when I am going to the post.

He salutes me in his usual manner, bringing his hand to his forehead. Sometimes he stops and asks me:

'How goes it?'

'All right,' I say to him, 'thank you.'

And we go off in opposite directions, I passing General Sartorio's wood, and he going by the lane which leads to the Casa Tonda.

Occasionally I meet Magna Maria. She is in deep mourning because Barba Tommaso has died. She waves to me from a distance and smiling shows her long white teeth.

Occasionally I meet Gemmina, who cuts me, and sometimes I meet Raffaella with Pepè.

Raffaella greets me and stops me.

She says, 'How sorry I am that you and Tommasino have not married.'

I say nothing and fondle Pepè's hair.

She says, 'I am sorry because I think you are very nice. Tommasino is nice, too.'

I say, 'Yes.'

She looks and looks at me with her large black curious eyes, trying to understand.

But she draws away and leaves me, to run after Pepè. She waves a hand to me in the distance.

As for Giuliana Bottiglia, I never see her. She is up there in her big house with three menservants and a gardener. They say, in the village, that Gigi goes to bed with the gardener and the menservants. With his wife, not much.

Signora Bottiglia says to my mother, 'Giuliana and Gigi, it's quite thrilling to see them, they are so happy.' She says, 'Gigi is so good, so good. He is always bringing her some present, from Paris, or from London. A crocodile handbag from Paris, absolutely lovely.'

'And from London?' asks my mother.

'From London, a silver tea-set. Teapot, sugar bowl and milk jug, three pieces.'

'Lovely,' says my mother.

'Pure Georgian, authentic,' says Signora Bottiglia.

'Georgian? From Georgia?'

'Georgia, of course not! Georgian, George—' explains Signora Bottiglia.

'Who is George?'

'Some king.'

My mother comes home and says to my father,

'The fact is, with this Gigi Sartorio one cannot make

out whether he is a pervert or not. It seems that he is fond of his wife, if one listens to Netta. Yet in the village they say that he has an understanding with the gardener. The gardener, I have seen him, is very ugly —he has long bristles in his nose.'

She says, after thinking it over for a bit,

'But perhaps he is very virile.'

It was October once again.

We were coming back, my mother and I, from La Vigna, where we had been to see how the grape-harvest was getting on. We were coming back and my mother walked very very slowly. I was a few steps ahead of her, carrying a basket of moscado grapes on my arm.

It was almost nightfall and beginning to be cold. The lamps were lit in the village. The ground on the path had become hardened and the grass was faded and damp. There was a decided nip in the air, probably snow would be coming soon.

My mother said, 'I have got a crick in my neck. I wonder why. It cannot be the wind; it must be rather that I turned too sharply when the woman called to me.'

She said, 'This new woman of ours—I can never remember the name—it is Drusbalda. They have strange fancies for names, in the country.'

She said, 'They don't seem bad. But they are not overclean. The house, I have seen it, was not very clean. They offered me coffee, and it has turned to vinegar in my stomach.

'Perhaps the cup was not clean. I drank it with some reluctance.

'Once of these days,' she said, 'I will go and visit Giuliana to see the tea-set.'

She said, 'I wonder how Giuliana actually managed to get married, when she is much more stupid than the other sisters.'

She said, 'It is always the stupid ones that get married—the girls.'

She said, 'I didn't go, you know, to Barba Tommaso's funeral. You were at Lambrate. Your father went with Aunt Ottavia. I, no. I was sorry not to go, because of Magna Maria. But I hadn't the strength; I did not feel I could shake hands with Purillo.'

She said, 'I never saw Purillo any more after it was broken off. I don't talk to you about it, because your father does not wish it. But I am sure it was Purillo's fault. It was he that set Tommasino against us.'

She said, 'Tommasino is a weak thing, a poor character. In the long run it is as well that you did not marry him. He is weak, he has no character, no definite personality. Down there at the works, he has no precise function either. He sits there behind a desk, because he is Balotta's son, and poor Vincenzino's brother. Now, Vincenzino—yes, he was authoritative, a strong character. Still, you see even for him marriage turned out badly. It is true that it was his wife's fault, that Catè.'

She said, 'So then Tommasino, because of his weak character, listened to Purillo. He must have told him —Purillo, I mean— to look for a girl with more money and no Socialists in the family.'

She said, 'Because, you know, they, those who own the factories, are always terrified of the Socialists. Inevitably. They make a pretence of liking them, of course. But it is not so. As soon as they get wind of them, they run away like hares, and good-bye. It is so nowadays. Once perhaps no, it was different. For example, old Balotta was a Socialist, certainly he was.'

She said, 'But your father does not wish me to talk of this to you. This has been a very great disappointment to us. Your father remains silent, but I know he is always thinking about it. He would like us to move now to Cignano. He has come to hate the village.'

She said, 'If we go to live at Cignano, I shall have Olga's company, Nino Conversi's daughter. I saw her the other day in the piazza, and she told me she will be very glad if we come. She has a girl of your age, she could play tennis. She does play, I think. And there is a boy, as well.

'She told me we can rent the apartment over the chemist's shop. It belongs to Pupazzina's father, Nebbia's widow, poor little thing.'

She said, 'As for our house here, I should let it. We shall certainly have to sell the dining-room suite, which takes up too much room. I am sorry about that, because it was my papa's.'

She said, 'However, I should always send for the meat here, once a week. It is much cheaper here. If I dispose of the dining-room suite, I shall buy a refrigerator. Giuliana has one, and they are very pleased with it.'

She said, 'However, butter and cheese are better at Cignano. They make those round cheeses, small round pieces salted. They are delicious.'

She said, 'Cignano lies rather lower, Cignano suits my blood pressure better.

'I wonder if she will be willing—Antonia, I mean,' she said, '—to come to Cignano.

'I wonder if she won't get it into her head that the air is bad for her.

'In any case if she does not come, I can do without. With the refrigerator and so many conveniences, what need is there of a servant?

'That apartment over the chemist's is small, but it is a gem. I have not seen it, Olga told me about it, this daughter of Nino's.'

She said, 'It means that if we are a bit cramped, you can sleep with Aunt Ottavia. The aunt does not worry you at all; it is enough to provide her with a book, and one hears nothing more from her.'

She said, 'I wonder if there will be fitted wardrobes. I wonder if there is a place for my chest of drawers.

'Now, as soon as we get home, I am going to take my temperature. I may easily have a bit of fever.

'I wonder if I should take an aspirin. I don't digest it as a rule. It is like lead in my stomach.

'The only drawback with that apartment over the chemist's is that the train passes very near. I sleep so lightly, how shall I ever drop off.

'I wonder if the chemist's bell will wake us in the night. I wonder if it rings loudly.

'But it will be convenient to have the chemist's shop beneath us. One will only have to go down a few steps if we need anything.

'I wonder if they keep the stuff that I take for my blood pressure at the chemist's in Cignano.'

THE END